Ralph Tate

A Plain and Easy Account of the Land

and freshwater mollusks of Great Britain

Ralph Tate

A Plain and Easy Account of the Land
and freshwater mollusks of Great Britain

ISBN/EAN: 9783337390990

Printed in Europe, USA, Canada, Australia, Japan

Cover: Foto ©Andreas Hilbeck / pixelio.de

More available books at **www.hansebooks.com**

A PLAIN AND EASY ACCOUNT OF

THE LAND AND FRESH-WATER
MOLLUSKS

OF GREAT BRITAIN;

CONTAINING DESCRIPTIONS, FIGURES, AND A FAMILIAR ACCOUNT
OF THE HABITS OF EACH SPECIES.

BY

RALPH TATE, F.G.S., F.A.S.L.,

EX-SECRETARY AND HONORARY CORRESPONDING MEMBER OF THE BELFAST
FIELD CLUB; LATE LECTURER ON NATURAL SCIENCE UNDER THE
COMMITTEE OF LECTURES, DUBLIN.

LONDON:
ROBERT HARDWICKE, 192, PICCADILLY, W.
1866.

COX AND WYMAN,
ORIENTAL, CLASSICAL, AND GENERAL PRINTERS,
GREAT QUEEN STREET, W.C.

PREFACE.

SLUGS and Snails! What interest can there be in such slimy, crawling things, from which we turn away in disgust? Yet these humble creatures are far from uninteresting to those who devote a little leisure to their examination. Many of our leading Naturalists acquired a taste for the pursuits of natural history, when but youths, in collecting and studying them.

We are only familiar with the common species of Snails, and the natural history of the majority of them is imperfectly known to us. There is here, then, a field of research open to lovers of nature.

In order to render this little volume instructive and interesting, as well to the general reader as to the young student, a familiar

account has been given of the habits of each
well-known species of our Land and Fluviatile
Mollusca; and whilst the scientific character of
the work has been uniformly sustained, all
unnecessary complexities have been carefully
avoided.

The classification adopted is that which is
employed by modern Zoologists. The specific
terms are those that have been long familiar to
home Naturalists. A few changes, however,
have been introduced, consisting in the restora-
tion of the older and equally well-known names.

The generic name *Helicella* is substituted for
that of *Zonites,* the latter name having been
generally, but erroneously, used in place of the
former.

R. T.

CONTENTS.

CHAPTER I.

CHAPTER II.

CHAPTER III.

CHAPTER IV.

MOLLUSKS.

CHAPTER I.

INTRODUCTION.

OBJECT AND NATURE OF ZOOLOGICAL CLASSIFICATION.
—CLASSES OF THE MOLLUSCOUS ANIMALS.

ANIMALS differ very much from one another not only in their form, size, and habits, but also in their internal structure; and we intuitively group them according to their resemblances and differences, and give to each group a certain distinctive or characteristic name. From childhood our minds have been engaged, consciously or unconsciously, in the observation of natural objects, noting their shapes and qualities, and rudely comparing and classifying them. The differences of internal structure have led naturalists to divide the animal kingdom into five divisions, each division being distinguished by some striking peculiarity of

B   *

structure, the animals comprised in each being constructed upon a plan differing from that of any of the other divisions. These primary groups, which are called sub-kingdoms, are as follows :—

1. Back-boned animals, termed *Vertebrata,* exemplified in beasts, birds, reptiles, and fishes.

2. Jointed animals, termed *Annulosa;* as insects, crabs, worms, &c.

3. Soft-bodied animals, termed *Mollusca;* as the common garden snail, the oyster, and cuttle-fish.

4. Hollow-intestined animals, termed *Cœlenterata;* as the sea-anemone, the coral polype.

5. Jelly animals, termed *Protozoa;* as infusory animalcules and the sponge.

The creatures living in our land and fresh-water shells, which form the subject of the present volume, belong to the group of soft-bodied animals, to which the term *Mollusca* is applied. They have, as the name implies, soft and fleshy bodies, not divided into segments, without bones or jointed limbs, enveloped in a muscular coat called the mantle, and the shell with which they are commonly protected is composed of either one or two, rarely more, pieces : the bodies of some are naked. The cuttle-fish and slug are examples which will give a general notion of the naked forms. The shelled species are familiar to us. The nervous system of the molluscous animals presents very marked peculiarities: in the back-boned and jointed animals, the principal mass of the nervous system, comprising the brain and spinal column, forms a continuous trunk throughout the length of the body, from which the nerves branch off at determinate points; whereas in the soft-bodied animals, the nervous system is composed of two or more pairs of brain-like masses scattered throughout the body, and united by cords of nerve-substance, which also send off nerves to the several parts of the body.

The sub-kingdom Mollusca admits of a very ready division into minor groups or *classes*. Thus we have cuttle-fishes, sea snails, land snails, bivalves, &c. In the language of the naturalist, the cuttle-fishes are the *Cephalopoda*, or head-footed mollusks; the sea snails are the *Gasteropoda*, or belly-footed mollusks; the land snails somewhat resemble the sea snails, but breathe air instead of water, and are hence termed *Pulmonifera*; the bivalves, as the mussel and oyster, are the *Conchifera*. There are four other classes of the Mollusca, but which, to-gether with the cuttle-fishes, do not come into the scope of the present subject, because they are all marine; so that all our land and fresh-water mollusks belong to the three classes, *Conchifera, Gasteropoda,* and *Pulmonifera.*

The ordinary bivalves (*Conchifera*)—as . the oyster, mussel, and cockle — are all aquatic animals, and by far the greater number of them live in the sea. They breathe by means of two pairs of gills in the form of plates or laminæ, and hence are also called *Lamellibranchiata;* they are, moreover, destitute of any distinct head, and are inclosed in a shell, composed of two pieces or valves.

The snail-like animals have a distinct head, provided with eyes, horns or tentacles, and a mouth armed with cutting jaws ; the under side of the body forms a single muscular foot, on which the animal creeps. The body is usually protected by a shell composed of one piece. Among these. belly-footed animals some live in the water, and breathe by means of gills,—these are the true *Gasteropoda;* others live on the land, as the snail and slug, and have the respiratory organ in the form of a lung,—these are comprised in the class *Pulmonifera.* Some, indeed, inhabit our fresh waters ; but, unlike the true fresh-water Gasteropods, they are compelled to come to the surface to breathe the air, and are not capable of suffering a long immersion in the water.

To pursue the scheme of classification. Each

class contains *orders,* and the orders are sub-
divided into *families;* each family is subdivided
into *genera,* and each genus contains one or
more *species.* The animal kingdom is composed
of individuals; but among these there are a certain
number which have a close resemblance to each
other, and are recognizable by a character which
is constant and definite. Such groups of individuals constitute what naturalists call *species.*
In familiar language, we speak of these in such
general terms as the horse, the oyster, the garden
snail, &c.,—meaning no horse in particular, no
oyster, no garden snail in particular. Let us
examine this matter more closely. Let us collect
a number of snails from a garden; we see that
they form a natural group, for they are all
characterized by a yellowish-coloured shell, beautifully banded with brown. This assemblage of
individuals with like characters we call "the
garden snail." Let us generalize still further
and higher, and extend our sphere of collection
to the neighbouring wood. We now find that
there are other undoubted snails, but which
evidently form a group distinct from "the
garden snail," for all their shells are of much
smaller size, and are clothed with hairs; from
which latter character we may appropriately call
them "the hairy snail." Observe that we have
naturally spoken of these two groups under the

common term "snail"—in Latin, *helix*. Now
the name employed to designate this assemblage
of species is the generic one. We distinguish
" the garden snail " by a further name, which is
the specific one, because it points out the species
or particular snail among the general assemblage
of snails. Thus the garden snail is known
among naturalists as *Helix hortensis;* that is,
Helix, a snail, and *hortensis*, of the garden.
The second species is *Helix hispida*, the hairy
or hispid snail.

A difficulty that meets us early in our examination of these animals, is the variation of form,
colour, and size among them. Now in the case
of the oyster, we are all familiar with the numerous variety of shapes that the shell of this
mollusk presents, yet we do not fail to recognize
them as belonging to the mollusk in question.
In the case of less familiar species, the difficulty
increases ; and we must here try to form a series,
with the normal or usual form as a centre, so as
to include the extremes of variation. In most
cases this is practicable. In a few instances
varieties have been produced, which have become fixed or permanent; that is to say, the peculiarities which distinguish the variety have
been perpetuated or handed down from generation to generation.

The principal causes of variation in shells are

abundance or scarcity of food, differences of habitat, &c. Thus, the shell of the large pond snail, *Limnæa stagnalis,* becomes more length-ened, tapering, and thinner, when the animal lives in running water, with only vegetable food as a diet, than the shells of more favoured indi-viduals inhabiting stagnant ponds, which fare more sumptuously upon dead dogs and other animals.

Classification is, then, an arrangement of all beings according to a certain order, by means of which objects are reunited into groups, recog-nizable by determinate characters, which, in their turn, are reunited into other groups of a still more comprehensive character. We have thus the ANIMAL KINGDOM subdivided into SUB-KINGDOMS; these sub-kingdoms are further sub-divided into CLASSES; and these classes, again, into ORDERS, FAMILIES, GENERA, and SPECIES.

"The practical utility of such a classification is easily seen by comparing it with the address of a letter. So it is with the naturalist, who by his classifications arrives speedily to the groups to which the animal belongs."*

If, for example, he wished to define a *garden snail,* without resorting to such means, he would be forced to compare his description with that of

* M. Milne-Edwards.

350,000 different animals. But if he says that the *garden snail* is a *molluscous* animal of the class *Pulmonifera*, of the family *Helicidæ*, of the genus *Helix*,—by the first he excludes all the vertebrated, annulated, coral-like, and jelly-like animals from his comparison; by the second, he excludes the bivalves, the water-breathing snails, and cuttle-fishes; by the third, he distinguishes the garden snail from the slugs, pond snails, and the like; and having arrived at the genus to which it belongs, a few distinguishing characters in addition will enable him to determine the species. Further, if the classification be based upon natural and not upon artificial characters, then it expresses the relationship of the species; for from the foregoing scheme of classification, it will be observed that differences in structure in the animals become less and less as we ascend in the scale of subdivision. Thus, for example, animals belonging to the same family, but of different genera, differ less from each other than animals belonging to different families.

The subject will be treated according to the following plan :—

The characters of each class will be studied by a full examination of the internal structures, as well as of the external or shelly parts, of a typical species of each. Technical terms, which we shall be compelled to use in describing each species, will here be fully explained and illustrated. The characters of the families and genera will be first defined, giving their resemblances and differences, and then the species contained in each genus will receive the lion's share of attention. Here we purpose to give a short description of the animal and its shell, so that we may be able to distinguish the species from others, followed by an account of its habits, where it may be sought for, and how the prize may be secured; in fact, all the incidents of its short but interesting life history will be given. Analytical tables, however, based on artificial characters, to facilitate a ready determination of the species and genera, will doubtless be found useful.

CHAPTER II.

BIVALVES (*Conchifera*).

I.—STRUCTURE OF THE PAINTERS' MUSSEL (*Unio pictorum*).

THE most common of the fresh-water bivalves is the swan mussel, an ordinary tenant of our rivers, streams, and ponds, lying half-buried in the mud. We select, however, the less widely distributed Painters' Mussel, as a type of the bivalves for study; because the characters of the class are better exhibited by it than by the swan mussel.

Let us first glance at the characters afforded by the shelly covering. The *shell* is at once seen to be composed of two pieces or *valves;* one is applied to the *left* side of the body of the mussel, and the other to the *right:* the valves are equal, and the shell is therefore said to be *equivalve.* The line along which the two valves are joined is the *hinge,* and that part in its vicinity, because it covers the back of the animal, is called the *dorsal region;* that opposite to it, the *ventral region.* The rounded margin is the *anterior margin* (fig. 1) ; and the pointed, the *posterior*. The prominent part of each valve near the hinge is the *umbo, u,* which, when it is in the middle, the shell is said to be *equilateral ;* but in the painters' mussel, we observe that the portion of the shell lying in the front of the umbo is shorter than that behind it, and the shell in this case is said to be *inequilateral.* Behind the umbo is a ridge, composed of a horny elastic substance, called the *ligament, l,* which is a mechanical contrivance by which the valves are opened. The depressed space in front of the umbo is the *lunule.* The *length* of the shell is measured from the anterior to the posterior side ; its *breadth* is the perpendicular distance from the umbo to the front ; its *thickness* is the diameter through the closed valves. Externally the valves are marked by concentric *lines of growth,* which diverge from the umbo, which is the point from which the growth of the valve commences.

The shell is composed of layers of animal matter impregnated with carbonate of lime, and consists of three structures :—an outer horny layer, called the *epidermis,* which does not contain calcareous salts; and which may be removed by steeping the shell in an acid solution, when the epidermis alone remains. Under the microscope, it exhibits a cellular structure in some parts, and a granular in others. Beneath the horny layer is a stratum consisting of delicate prismatic cells of calcareous matter, and an internal layer, which is shining and pearly, and makes up nearly the whole thickness of the shell. This latter, or *nacreous* layer, consists of folded plates of carbonate of lime, which, by refracting the light, give rise to that characteristic pearly lustre of the interior : this portion, when polished, forms " mother-of-pearl." For the microscopic examination of the shell structure, sections are necessary ; but in place of these, thin edges of broken portions of the shell may be employed. The shell grows partly by addition to the margin and partly to the interior.

In the interior of the shell, the following markings and parts are to be distinguished :—

The *umbonal cavity* corresponding to the umbo.

The *hinge-line* of the right valve presents a prominence or *tooth* (Plate II., fig. 2) towards the front, which fits into a depression between two teeth in the left valve. On the posterior part of the hinge-line of each valve is developed an elongated tooth : these are said to be *lateral;* but when they are situated beneath the umbo, as in the fresh-water *cyclas*, they are termed **cardinal**. On the inner surface of the valves are seen two impressions or distinct pits, one near the posterior (*a, a'*), and one near the anterior sides in each valve, made by two strong muscles extending internally from one valve to the other.

These adductor muscular scars, as they are called, are connected by a faintly impressed line following the curvature, and near the front of the valve: this is the impression left by the attachment of the muscles of the mantle. Near to the adductor muscular scars, but a little further from the edge of the shell, are situated the impressions of the muscles that move the foot.

Figure 1 represents the right valve of the shell removed so as to disclose the animal. It is necessary for all dissections to remove one of the valves. This may be readily accomplished by first killing the animal by hot water, when the valves will gape open. Forcing them now wider apart, the muscles which close the valves may be then readily seen, as white cords, which must be cut with a pair of scissors. The whole body of the animal is covered by a thin fleshy envelope, termed the *mantle*, which consists of two lobes, joined at the back, but free in front. The disposition of the lobes has been well compared to the " covers of a book when it is placed on its edge with the back uppermost." Each lobe of the mantle corresponds with a valve of the shell, and is attached to it in front by a series of muscles, which produce the mantle-line of impressions. The mantle extends as a free portion beyond the muscles to the edge of the shell, which portion is much thickened, and secretes the shell. The lobes of the mantle are united near the posterior margin and pierced by two orifices; the upper one is called the *anal opening* (fig. 1, *v*), the lower one the *branchial opening, b.*

The *digestive organs.*—The mouth (*o*) is a horizontal opening situated anteriorly just above the foot, between two pairs of soft flattened lips (*t*);

Dorsal margin.

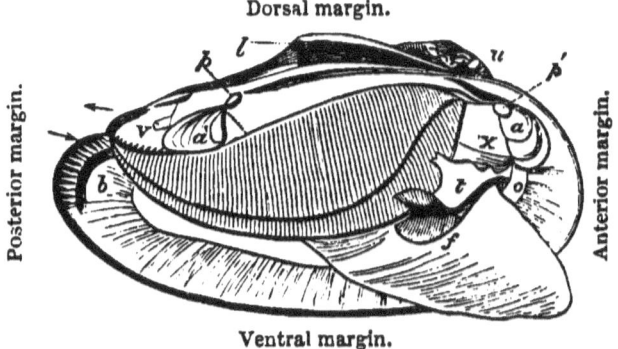

Ventral margin.

Fig. 1.

it is rather difficult to find, but may be discovered by tracing the lips to their insertions, between which the mouth is situated. The mouth opens immediately into a stomach, which contains a cylindrical jelly-like body, termed the *crystalline style*, whose function is not known. The intestinal canal is a narrow tube wound around a large liver, and after passing through the heart, is continued along the back to the vent (*v*), which is situated near the anal orifice: the excremental matters are carried away by the water which had passed over the gills.

The *circulatory apparatus* consists of a heart composed of two auricles and a ventricle, and may be readily discovered, as it is situated in the middle portion of the back of the animal, under the hinge; its beatings, which are about six or eight in a minute, are easily seen under the large bag, or *pericardium,* containing the heart. The heart continues to beat for a long time after the valves have been opened. The blood of shell-fish is white, or nearly colourless; and so essential is the red character of blood deemed by the vulgar, that it appears to them little less than an abuse of language to apply the term to the nearly colourless fluid of the mussel; but it possesses all the essential properties of blood, flows in a similar circle of vessels, and answers the same purposes in the system. The blood is propelled by the contraction of the ventricle into the arteries, and after supplying the waste of the body, is collected as venous blood by the veins from the capillary extremities; and after becoming aërated in the gills, is received by the gill-veins and conveyed as arterial blood to the auricles; from thence it passes into the ventricle, to be again distributed through the whole system.

The *respiratory organs* are gills, consisting of two membranous plates, attached to each lobe of the mantle; each plate consists of two folds of its membrane, and is pierced by innumerable holes, which are beset with *vibratile cilia* ; by the action of these extremely delicate filaments, a current of water is produced, setting in by the branchial orifice (fig. 1, *b*), which is surrounded by a fringe of sensitive tentacular organs, and sweeping over the gills, it is propelled towards the mouth (*o*), and passes out by the anal orifice (*v*) : by this agency, the layer of water in contact with the gills is thus renewed, and food is also brought to the mouth.

These currents may be rendered distinct by introducing some powdered indigo into a basin of water containing a fresh-water mussel.

The branchial currents are most conveniently exhibited by the Zebra mussel, possessing, as it does, two prominent siphons (fig. 2). The inhalent siphon is densely fringed, and if the processes be touched, the orifice closes, and the siphon is at once retracted. When unmolested, a current flows steadily into the one orifice, whilst another current rises up from the other, as indicated by the arrows.

The wonderful activity of the cilia is a most striking spectacle ; a magnifying power of about 120 diameters is amply sufficient to obtain a general view of the movements. A small portion of the gill must be carefully spread out on a glass slide, with a little water, and covered by a glass disk ; or the animalcule-cage may be conveniently used. A much higher magnifying power is required to observe the movements of each cilium.

The *nervous system* consists of three pairs of white nervous centres, called *ganglia*, from which the nerves radiate. Two ganglionic masses (the *cerebral*) are situated on the sides of the mouth, and are united to form a ring around the gullet; they are connected with two others (*pedal*) in the foot, and with those (the *branchial*) placed a little below the posterior adductor muscle near the anal orifice. This distribution of the nervous centres is eminently characteristic of the sub-kingdom Mollusca.

Organs of Sense.—The organs of hearing are two little sacs, situated on a pair of nerves arising from the ganglia of the foot, and contain a fluid in which is suspended a small calcareous body or *otolith*. The organs of sight are in the form of black dots, or *ocelli*, along the margin of the mantle.

Muscular Organs.—The ventral portion of the body is prolonged to form a fleshy tongue-shaped foot (*f*), and has some analogy with the Gasteropods: this locomotive organ is large, flexible, and muscular, and capable of being protruded beyond the shell. Change of position is effected by the insertion of the foot beneath the shell, and, by being employed as a lever, the shell is jerked forward; or the extremity of the protruded foot is made a lever, and the animal draws itself forward. By means of the same organ, the animal can bury itself in the sand or mud, in which it lives. The pedal muscles (p, p') retract the foot.

The adductor muscles (a, a') are two in number, they extend from one valve to the other, and by their contraction the shell is closed; they are hence named *adductors*. On their relaxation, or if they be cut, the elasticity of the ligament comes into play, and the valves are opened. The term *dimyary* bivalves is applied to such, as the *Unio*, with two adductor muscles; the *monomyary* bivalves, as the oyster, have only one. The fresh-water Conchifera are all dimyarian bivalves.

Reproduction. — Each individual is male or female. The impregnated eggs, of which 200,000 are computed to be produced by each individual in the year, pass into the external folds of the gills, which during the breeding season in early spring are broad and thick : here they are hatched, and the young remain for some time. The embryos are very unlike the parent, and have been described as parasites under the name of *Glochidium*. They have a triangular shell provided with serrated hooks, and have but one adductor muscle, and a long slender byssal filament. In this condition they have been found attached to the tails of fish, floating wood, &c. We see in this a provision for the dispersion of these sedentary bivalves. Nothing is known of the history of the embryo from this stage until it assumes the form of the adult.

As the Swan Mussel (*Anodon cygneus*) may be more within the reach of many of my readers, I would inform them that it does not possess a distinct lunule nor inter-locking teeth, nor are the muscular impressions so distinct; but in all other respects it resembles *Unio*.

The *Food* of bivalves consists of *infusoria*, *diatoms*, and vegetable matter, brought to the mouth by the portion of the branchial current, which is projected in that direction.

Collecting, &c.—The majority of the Conchifera live buried vertically in the mud : they may be collected by dredging with a kind of perforated tin saucepan, about six inches across, and furnished with a hollow handle, so as to receive the end of a stout walking-stick.

After making a scoop with the tin, it should be shaken, keeping the mouth just above the surface of the water, for fear of washing out any of the shelly contents; by this means the mud and fine sand pass out through the perforations of the tin, and the shells and gravel are retained. The large shells may be bagged, the smaller ones placed in glass bottles or tin boxes. To prepare them for the cabinet, the shells should be first cleaned with a brush, and after being immersed in boiling water, the animals may be removed. The interiors of the shells should be wiped dry, and the valves closed, and tied with a *moist* tape or cotton; they should now be allowed to dry slowly, for if heated too much they are apt to crack.

II.—DESCRIPTION OF SPECIES.

THE fresh-water bivalves of Great Britain are comprised in the three families—*Mytilidæ, Unionidæ*, and *Cycladidæ*.

FAMILY MYTILIDÆ (MUSSELS).

This family is typified by the common marine mussel (*Mytilus edulis*) of our coasts, and is represented in our fresh waters by

DRIESSENA POLYMORPHA (*the Zebra Mussel*) (Pl. IV., fig. 25).—This bivalve closely resembles the common mussel; the shell is equi-valve, wedge-shaped, rounded behind; the umbones are placed at the anterior end; the valves are sharply keeled in the middle. The principal differences between this genus and *Mytilus* are as follows:—In *Mytilus* the mantle is open, in *Driessena* closed; in *Mytilus* the gills adhere through their whole length, in *Driessena* the extremities are free. In *Driessena* the anterior adductor muscle is supported on a triangular shelf below the beak.

The mantle of *Driessena* is united all round, with the exception of three apertures (fig. 2)—one the anal orifice, which is prolonged into a very small tube; a second, the branchial orifice, furnished with a prominent siphon or tube, which is fringed on the inside.

The Zebra Mussel is an attached bivalve, like its brethren of the sea; the foot (*f*) is very imperfectly developed, giving place to a gland, which secretes the material of the threads with which it attaches itself to stones, timber, and shells; these threads are termed the *byssus* (*b*); and the third opening in the united

Fig. 2.—*Driessena polymorpha.*

mantle lobes is for the passage of these mooring cables. The epidermis of the shell is yellowish-brown, with undulating streaks, or zebra-like markings of dark brown.

This mussel was first discovered by Pallas, in the different rivers of Russia and also in the Caspian Sea; and from the great variety of forms presented by this species, he designated it under the name *Mytilus polymorphus.* Van Beneden, in 1835, showed it to differ from *Mytilus,* and constituted for it the genus *Driessena,* de-

rived from the name of M. Driessenus, an apothe-
cary of Mazeyk, from whom the former received
in the year 1822 a collection of these mussels
alive, from a canal near Maestricht. But as
early as 1824 Mr. J. de C. Sowerby called
attention to its occurrence in the Commercial
Docks on the Thames, where it was already
abundant, and used by anglers as a bait for
perch, whither it had been brought attached to
timber from Eastern Europe.

The mode by which it has been introduced is
evidently by its being affixed to the logs of timber before they were stowed in the ship's hold,
for it has been seen adhering to them before they
were unloaded, and not that it had attached itself
to the ship's bottom, and so been conveyed. The
former mode of transport is the more rational, as
the bivalve can survive a removal from the water
for several weeks, especially under such favourable conditions as prevail in the moist hold of a
ship.

In 1833 it was found in vast abundance in the
Clyde and Forth Canal, Glasgow; in 1834 it
appeared in the Union Canal, Edinburgh; and in
1836 it was found in considerable numbers on
the piers of the bridge which crosses the Nen
at Fotheringay, in which locality it had been introduced from Wisbeach, on timber, since 1828.
In 1837, the late Mr. Hugh Strickland found it

completely established on the beds of gravel in
the river Avon, at Evesham, and also in the canal
between Warwick and Birmingham, and in the
canals near Wednesbury, in Staffordshire. He
remarked that, as its propagation was so aston-
ishingly rapid, it would become in a few years
one of our commonest British shells. This has
proved so true, that not only has it found its way
throughout England, literally paving with its
shells the beds and sides of our navigable rivers
and canals, but it has even taken up its quarters
in the water-pipes of London, Manchester, &c.

The Zebra Mussel made its appearance in the
neighbourhood of Gloucester a few years after
the opening of the Gloucester and Berkeley Canal,
and has increased in numbers to such an extent,
that it may be said to line the banks from the
edge of the water to a considerable depth,
throughout its entire length of sixteen miles. It
appears in every available inch of space, from
the water-line to the depth of fifteen or sixteen
feet, upon the dock walls at Gloucester.

It is very tenacious of life and exceedingly
prolific, provided the locality is favourable.

This mollusk is evidently sensible to light,
which it would usually avoid, as exemplified in
its occurrence in such prodigious numbers in
water-pipes. If when the animal is at rest, with
the shell partly open, an object is suddenly

brought before it, the valves are at once closed, or partially so. On being introduced into the aquarium, it at once reconciles itself to its new abode, mooring itself by its threads to the stones, or the sides of the glass. Young individuals are harder to please, exhibiting their dissatisfaction by their peregrinations, making the circuit of the aquarium before selecting a resting-place; but on finding a suitable spot, they follow the example of their seniors and secrete a byssus, and there remain fixed for life.

The present species is now found in almost every part of Europe, in canals, tanks, running streams, and rivers, attaching itself by its byssus of strong threads to stones, the live shells of *Anodon*, and the dead ones of their own species, wood piles, or brickwork. In docks it luxuriates beneath the floating timber ; in canals it abounds beneath the shadow of bridges. It has not yet found its way into Ireland.

Extinct species of *Driessena* inhabited the fresh waters of the Isle of Wight during the Upper Eocene epoch. *D. polymorpha* is, however, absent from the newer Tertiaries of this country.

1.

Vincent Brooks, Imp.

FRESH-WATER MUSSELS.

Family Unionidæ.

This group contains several genera of exclusively fresh-water habits. There are only two European genera, which are also British,—*Unio* and *Anodon*, characterized by their oblong shells, the mantle-lobes free all round except at the posterior side, where the edge is bearded. *Anodon* is distinguished from *Unio* by the absence of teeth on the hinge-line; hence called *edentulous*.

The *Unionidæ* have all large shells; the animals bury themselves vertically in the mud of rivers, &c., the posterior side upwards. The exposed portion of the shell is usually encrusted with a calcareous deposit. The umbones, especially of *Unio*, are generally much eroded by the acids dissolved in the water. *Unios* are the most ancient of the fluviatile Mollusca. A *Unio* or *Anodon* appears in the Old Red Sandstone of Kilkenny. They characterize the fresh-water deposits of the Purbeck, Hastings Sands, Weald Clay, and Middle and Upper Eocene strata. A species, *U. littoralis*, now living in the north of France and Sicily, occurs in the fluviatile deposits at Clacton, Ilford, and Cropthorn. *U. pictorum*,

U. tumidus, and *Anodonta cygnea* are found with it.

UNIO TUMIDUS—(*the swollen Fresh-water Mussel*) (Pl. II., fig. 2)—(*Unio,* Lat., a pearl).—The shell is about three inches long and one and a half wide, oval, solid with a thick glossy dark brown epidermis. The umbones are prominent; the lunule is lanceolate and narrow; the ligament is short, thick, and prominent; the anterior side is rounded and regularly sloping towards the front; the posterior side wedge-shaped. The interior is bluish-white or salmon-colour.

It inhabits canals and slow-running rivers with a muddy bottom, burying itself in a vertical position more than one-half of its length. It extends as far north as Yorkshire.

UNIO PICTORUM—(*the Painters' Mussel*) (Pl. II., fig. 3).—The specific name originated in the use of these shells for holding colours by Dutch painters. The shell is less solid and of a more oblong form, and necessarily of greater proportionate width than that of *U. tumidus.* The epidermis is thin and beautifully coloured, of a shining greenish-yellow, banded with brown. The length is about two or three inches. It is associated with the last species.

UNIO MARGARITIFERUS—(*the Pearl or Black Mussel*) (Pl. III., fig. 15).—This species, also

called *Alasmodonta margaritifera*, is markedly
distinct from the other species; in its superior
size, often five and a half inches long and two
and a half wide, and one thick,—it is thus proportionately much longer and more compressed;
in its strong and pitch-black epidermis, and in
the adult specimens by the posterior tooth being
obsolete. The umbones are extensively eroded,
and the valves are narrowed in the middle. It
loves to lurk among the gravel and small stones
in the shallows of quick-flowing rivers or mountain streams. It is found in the North of England,
North and South Wales; near Ross, in the Wye;
Devonshire and Cornwall; in the rivers flowing
from the Scotch Highlands; and in many of the
North and South Irish rivers.

It burrows its shell somewhat obliquely, a
small portion of which is thus only exposed. A
diligent search is required to find it, as by the
growth of confervæ upon the little exposed portion, it cannot easily be distinguished from
amongst the surrounding stones.

It is very susceptible to the action of light,
opening the valves on a hot sunny day; but if the
sun be overcast they remain closed. Country
boys wade for them, or take them by thrusting
the end of a long slender rod into the partially
open shell, which closes upon it, and the prize is
thus dragged to shore.

The Pearl Mussel enjoys a reputation as one of the few British bivalves which contain the beautiful production whose name this species bears. The other *Unios* and the *Anodon* occasionally yield pearls, as also the marine mussel (*Mytilus edulis*) and the oyster.

Pearls are of the same nature as the nacreous layer of the shell, and are abnormal secretions of the mantle, composed of alternate layers of animal membrane and calcareous matter, developed around some foreign body,—a grain of sand, a parasite, or an unfertilized ovum.

The great Linnæus owed in part his elevation to nobility to a discovery of causing this fresh-water mussel to produce pearls at pleasure. This was accomplished, it is conjectured, by boring small holes through the shell and introducing a particle of sand, which would become a nucleus round which a pearl would be developed ; but the artificial production of pearls had been long known to the Chinese. The *Avicula margaritifera* of the Indian seas is the most famous for pearls.

Pearls have been associated with the name of Britain from the very earliest known times. Suetonius gives as the reason for Cæsar's expedition into Britain, the search for pearls, which Pliny seems to confirm, saying that Cæsar gave a breast-plate covered with British pearls to Venus Genitrix, and hung it in her temple at Rome; he further adds that they (probably from *Mytilus edulis*) were small and ill-coloured, and Tacitus says the same; but the Venerable Bede, on the other hand, states that the British pearls were excellent and of all colours—reddish, pale violet, and green. In an old translation of Boetius, by Bellenden (1541), the following allusion is made to British pearls:—"In the horse mussillis are generit perlis. Thir mussillis airlie in the morning, when the lift is clear and temperate, openis thair mouthis a little aboue the watter, and maist gredelie swellis the dew of heaven, and aftir the measure of the dew they swellie, they conceive and bredis the perle." Camden, still later, in his "Britannica," speaks of the shell-fish of the little river Irt, in Cumberland, "that they, by a kind of irregular motion, take in the dew and produce pearls."

The Pearl Mussel was formerly an object of considerable fisheries in our own country, as it is now in some parts of Germany. So, also, the common mussel, a pearl fishery of which continued to exist up to a very recent period at the mouth of the river Conway, in North Wales. A patent was also granted early in the present century to fish for pearls at the mouth of the river Irt, in Cumberland. Higher up both rivers, however, the Unio has been at various

times also fished to a great extent for the orna-
mental excretions to which it is subject. The
pearls from *Mytilus edulis* are very much inferior in quality and size to those from the
Unio. Those of the Conway had great fame.
Extensive fisheries existed in the rivers of
Tyrone, Derry, Donegal, near Dundalk, near
Waterford, and in Kerry. In Scotland, the Tay
was the seat of a pearl fishery. "It is said,"
writes Captain Brown, "that the pearls sent
from thence to London from the year 1761 to
1764 were worth £10,000, and it is not uncommon at the present day to find pearls in the
Teith and Tay worth from £1 to £2 sterling
each." The var. *Roissyi* was formerly much
sought for in the Black River, Kirk Braddam,
Isle of Man, on account of its pearls.

ANODON CYGNEUS—(*the Swan Mussel*) (Pl. I.,
fig. 1)—attains a size considerably larger than
the *Unios*. The maximum size exceeds in length
eight and in breadth four and a half inches.
It is readily distinguished by its rather thin,
oval (truncated behind) shell, compressed in
the young, but becoming ventricose with age.
The epidermis is glossy, dull green, more or less
tinged with dusky, and slightly radiated; the
inside of the shell is bluish-white, pearly in young
and yellowish-white in old shells. The umbones

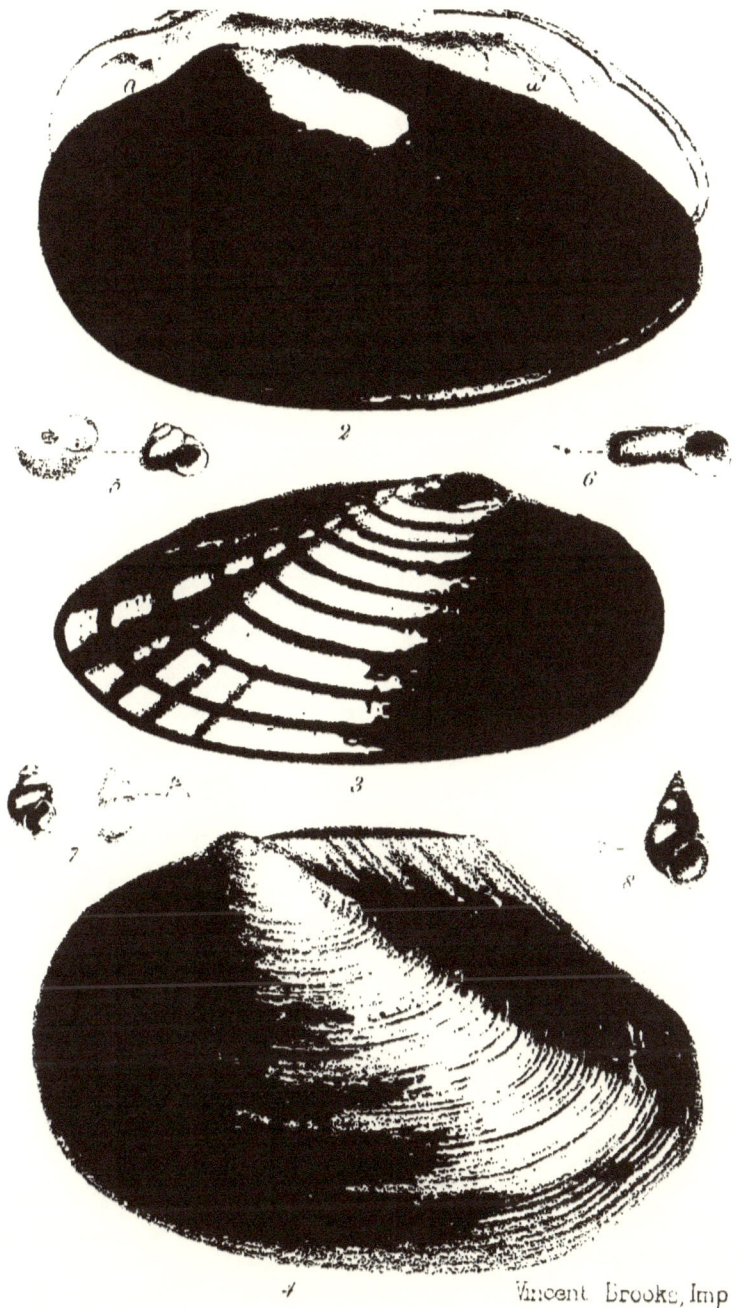

are very small and convex; the lunule is indistinct, and the hinge-line is without teeth.

The Swan Mussels live in lakes, ponds, canals, and muddy rivers, and are found in suitable localities throughout the kingdom.

Anodons vary very much, not only according to locality, but in the same waters; some of the numerous varieties should, it is thought, be more justly regarded as species. In ponds where there is plenty of food, and where the water is nearly stagnant, they become of large size, with ventricose thin shells, and are type forms; whilst in more rapid rivers, with pure clear water, with very little decomposing animal or vegetable matter, they are small and comparatively longer than *A. cygneus*, with compressed thick shells, and are the *A. anatinus* (Pl. II., fig. 4) of some authors; but all intermediate forms and sizes may be observed.

The manner of locomotion is slow and regular, leaving their tracks distinctly discernible in the soft mud. At Bottesford, on the Trent, where at high tides the water is salt, it is found in great abundance.

Anodons are thrown up in quantities on the shores of Lough Schur, co. Leitrim, where they are eaten by the peasantry. *Sliggaun* is the common name applied to the Swan Mussel in the North of Ireland.

Anodons furnish a very favourite repast for the herons, and crows feed upon them. Pennant says, "that when the shell is too hard for their bills, they will fly with it to a great height, drop the shell on a rock, and pick out the meat when the shell is fractured by the fall."

This species is invested with a mite (*Atax ypsilophora*), which is so tenacious of life that they survive an immersion in boiling water.

FAMILY CYCLADIDÆ.

The remaining British fluviatile bivalves belong to the family Cycladidæ, characterized by the mantle-lobes being united at the posterior side to form one or two prominent contractile respiratory siphons. The foot is large and tongue-like. The shells are small, thin, and sub-orbicular; the hinge-line with minute cardinal

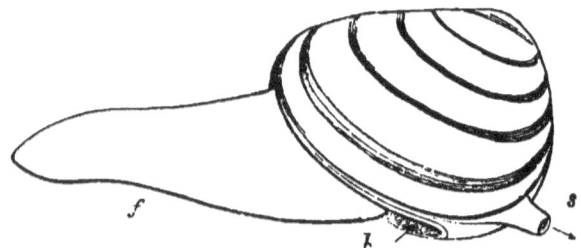

Fig. 3.—*Pisidium amnicum*, with its foot and siphon protruded.

and lateral teeth, two cardinals, and a lateral on each side, in the left valve; in the right, one cardinal, and two laterals on each side.

The family contains two British genera, *Cyclas* and *Pisidium;* the respiratory siphons are two in number in *Cyclas* (Pl. III., fig. 17); there is only one (fig. 3, *s*) in *Pisidium,* the branchial and pedal orifices being confluent (*b*). The shells of *Pisidium* are inequilateral, those of *Cyclas* rounded, and more or less equilateral.

GENUS CYCLAS.

There are five British species of this genus, the largest of which is

CYCLAS RIVICOLA—(*the River Cyclas*) (Pl. III., fig. 17).—The shell of this species is distinguished by its great size, its more oval form, the strong concentric ridges on the shell, and the prominent ligament. The oval equilateral shell is ten lines in length, seven in width, and five in thickness; the epidermis is thick, of a glossy reddish or greenish-brown, with two or three darker bands, strongly striated concentrically; the interior of the valves is whitish, with a bluish or yellowish tinge.

This species burrows in the mud of canals and slow-running rivers, in the southern and midland counties of England: it is plentiful in the docks and canals about London; it occurs in the Thames, above Chelsea; in the Medway at Maidstone; Kennet and Avon Canal, Wilts; Severn, at Wainlode; Tewkesbury; Newent,

Berkeley, and Combe Hill Canals, Gloucestershire; Oxford; Chester; York; Doncaster; &c.
It is a species of the newer Tertiaries.

CYCLAS CORNEA—(*the Horny Cyclas*) (Pl. III.,
fig. 18).—The shell of this species is not more
than half the size of the last, and more globular;
its length about six lines, breadth four, and thickness three and a half; equilateral, finely striated
concentrically, of a yellowish-brown colour, with
paler bands; ligament indistinct externally.

It varies very considerably: there are three
well-known varieties.—1. var. *flavescens* (Pl. III.,
fig. 16), with a smaller and rounder shell, the
body and shell straw- or lemon-coloured. 2.
Which is probably the fry of *C. cornea*, with a
small, nearly globular shell. 3. Gibbous at the
beaks, but thin or compressed towards the edges.

Few pools, ditches, or streams throughout the
United Kingdom are without this very interesting
bivalve. In summer it is found among the confervæ floating near the surface of the water; in
winter it buries itself in the mud.

No aquarium can be considered at all complete
without this interesting animal, whose habits are
so much at variance with the popular notions regarding the way in which mussels, cockles, and
other bivalves pass their days. It crawls readily
by the aid of its long foot, or ascends the sides
of the glass, and, on reaching the surface, moors

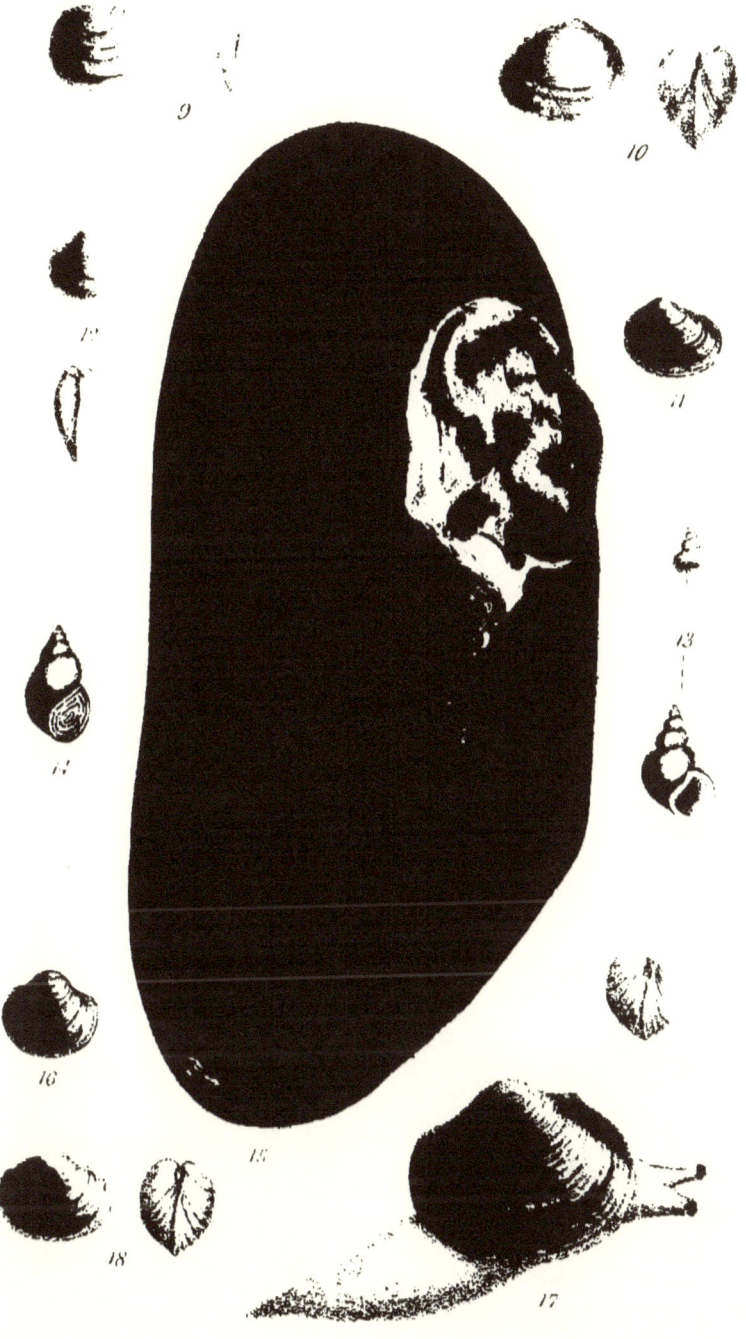

itself with the shell immersed and inverted, by glutinous threads, which are spun by the foot, or it may even be observed gliding along the surface of the water in an inverted position. It is very active, and climbs the submerged plants with great facility, among which it is usually found; it can suspend itself by its glutinous threads, which are of the nature of a byssus, as in the *Driessena* and *Mytilus.*

It thrives well and breeds in confinement; the fry are hatched in the gills, are but few in number (each gill containing not more than about six), and of different sizes, the largest varying from one-eighth to one-fourth the length of the parent.

The larvæ of a fluke (*Amphistoma subclavatum*) have been found on the surface of the body of this and other species of *Cyclas*, as also on the coil-shells (*Planorbis*). It is a newer Tertiary species.

CYCLAS PISIDIOIDES (Pl. III., fig. 9) is a recent addition to science; it was discovered, in 1856, in the Paddington Canal, near Kensal Green, London. It has much the appearance of a large *Pisidium;* hence its specific name. The adult shells are six lines long, five wide, and four thick. It is distinguished from *C. cornea* by its subtriangular shell, which is somewhat produced behind and slightly wrinkled concentrically.

The same locality supplied, at the same time, a species new to Britain,—

CYCLAS OVALIS—(*the Oval Cyclas*) (Pl. III., fig. 10)—is a species intermediate in size and form between *C. rivicola* and *C. cornea.* Average-sized specimens measure half an inch long, a quarter of an inch thick, and three-eighths wide. From *C. rivicola* it is distinguished by its oblong shape, its pale-drab colour, and fainter concentric striæ, and more markedly by its straight hinge-line. It has since been found in the Surrey Canal, at Exmouth, and in Lancashire. It occurs in marshes in the North of France.

CYCLAS LACUSTRIS—(*the Capped Cyclas*) (Pl. III., fig. 12).—The shell of this species contrasts strongly with those of the other Cyclads, in its sub-rhombic form, much compressed, thin, of a yellowish-white colour ; in the prominent umbones, which are narrow, and projecting like little caps, from which latter character it has also received the specific name *calyculata.*

The shell is small, delicate, and shining, four lines long, three wide, and one and a half thick.

From the extreme thinness and semitransparency of the shell, the young, the lamellated gills, and the pulsating heart may be easily seen within.

C. lacustris has much the same habits as *C.*

cornea, but exhibits greater activity than it does.

We quote a writer in the *Zoologist,* who gives in a few words the performances of this bivalve in confinement.

"When I first put them (*C. lacustris*) into water they immediately began to climb the sides of the glass. One of them also commenced crawling on the under surface of the water. Its foot was now spread out very widely, and while preparing for its exploit, it was apparently kept near the surface by a minute thread fastened to the sides of the glass. When it had left the side, its foot appeared to be depressed in the middle, so as to act as a kind of boat. I shook the tumbler, so as to fill the little vessel with water; but to my surprise it sunk, *not suddenly* but *gradually,* as if it were lowering itself by a thread attached to the surface of the water. They also appeared to give out a quantity of glutinous matter wherever they went, so much, that in about half an hour seven or eight were entangled and tied together by each other's trailing threads."

The capped Cycle inhabits ponds, canals, ditches, and lakes in the South and centre of England, becoming rare in the North; it is absent in Scotland, and is rare and local in Ireland, having been observed only near Dublin, Dundalk, Youghal, and Cork.

Genus Pisidium.

This genus is separated from *Cyclas* to receive the smaller species, which have inequilateral shells, and have only one siphonal tube; the incurrent aperture being confluent with that for the passage of the foot (see fig. 3, p. 32). They have much the same habits as *Cyclas,* and live in similar situations. It is very difficult to distinguish the species from each other, which, therefore, necessitates detailed descriptions of each. The largest and one easily recognized is—

Pisidium amnicum — *(inhabiting rivers)* (Pl. III., fig. 11).—The shell is triangular, deeply grooved concentrically, of a whitish-grey or pale brown; umbones very little produced; four lines long, one and a half thick, and three wide. It usually buries itself in the mud, but climbs by the aid of its long flexible foot among the aquatic plants. It is common, and universally distributed over Great Britain and Europe. It is fossilized in the newer Tertiaries.

Pisidium cinereum (Pl. IV., fig. 21) approaches the last, as regards size, more than any of the other species. Shell greyish, with one or two broad bands, more compressed and oval than the others of the genus, finely striated; umbones obtuse and prominent, sometimes slightly capped, like *Cyclas lacustris*. Length three lines, thickness one and a half, and width two and a half. In ditches and slow streams widely diffused.

PISIDIUM PULCHELLUM (Pl. IV., fig. 24) is the smallest of the genus, differs from the last in size, and is of a less triangular form. The shell is only one and a half lines long and wide, half a line thick, of a glossy white, sometimes greyish, finely and irregularly striated.

This handsome and well-marked species well merits its specific name (*pulchellus*, small and beautiful); it is universally distributed. It inhabits stagnant and running water, and at the same time and place may be found on submerged plants, and buried in the mud. It occurs in the newer Tertiaries.

Professor Macgillivray made the following observations on individuals of this species found in a ditch near Aberdeen :—" When advancing in the water, the animal opens its valves a little, places itself erect by means of the foot, which it gradually protrudes until it extends to a length and a half of the shell, but often to twice its length. When thus extended it is of a linear-oblong form, very little flattened, narrowed but rounder at the end. It then contracts, and drags the shell quickly forward; after which it is again extended, and again contracts. It is not always stretched out in a direct line, but is moved in an undulating manner, often from side to side, and appears to act as a tentaculum, as well as an organ of motion. The siphonal tube, which is at the same time extended and kept so, is short, cylindrical, truncate, and changes but little; sometimes, however, it is nearly elliptical; it never extends beyond a sixth of the length of the shell. A current is seen passing out of it, and minute dark particles frequently escape. In this manner the animal advances with considerable speed by jerks. At other times it ascends to the surface, where it proceeds in the same manner, with the shell reversed. The animal can advance equally with the shell inclined to either side; it can creep in any direction, on a level or inclined surface, and ascend or descend a perpendicular plane. On opening an individual in which young were seen, I found six lodged there. They were very large, much compressed, elliptical, with the umbones nearly central; the colour white; the surface beautifully glossed, and almost perfectly smooth. On being removed and placed in the water, some of them soon began to move in the same manner as the adults, but with the shell inclined on one side."

PISIDIUM HENSLOWIANUM (Pl. IV., fig. 19), named after Professor Henslow, is very closely allied to the last, which may be a variety of this, but easily known by the plate-like projection on each valve near the umbones.

It occurs in several localities in England and in South Wales; the only Irish locality recorded is Finnoe, co. Tipperary. It occurs in the newer Tertiaries.

PISIDIUM NITIDUM — (*the Shining Pisidium*) (Pl. IV., fig. 22).— Shell suborbicular, very shining, finely and regularly striated, with a few separate and deeper grooves around the obtuse and subcentral umbones. Length one-twelfth of an inch, width one-fifth less. The most obvious distinctive characters are its rounded outline, glossy and iridescent appearance, the strong concentric grooves on the umbonal region, which are more readily seen in young shells, and the funnel-shaped siphon with its plaited outer margin.

It is somewhat generally distributed in lakes, ponds, and pools. Mr. J. Thompson found it abundantly in a cold turfy deposit conveyed by a mountain stream to a pond near Belfast, and on *Utricularia vulgaris*, growing in stagnant pools. These places are of a very different nature, the pond at the former being supplied with clear spring water, and at an elevation of 600 feet above the sea; the latter but a few feet above it, and supplied only with rain-water.

PISIDIUM PUSILLUM—(*the Dwarf Pisidium*) (Pl.
IV., fig. 23).—The yellowish-white shell is oval,
less compressed than the last, very finely but irregularly striated ; the umbones nearly central ; the
posterior a very little more produced than the
rounder anterior side. It is the least inequilateral of the *Pisidia*. It is the most common of
the genus ; is universally distributed throughout
the country, inhabiting ponds, drains, ditches, &c.
It does not apparently require a constant supply
of water, being often found in marshy spots in
company with and adhering to the same stones
as the land mollusca inhabiting such places.
Mr. Thompson procured it in the North and
South of Ireland, among moss which was kept
moist only by the spray of waterfalls. It is found
in the newer Tertiary deposits.

PISIDIUM OBTUSALE (Pl. IV., fig. 20).—The shell
of this species is closely allied to that of *P. pusillum*
in its blunt, nearly central umbones, but is smaller
and much more ventricose ; the umbones are
rather prominent and very blunt. It is one of
the rarest of the genus, but occurs throughout
Great Britain. Mr. J. Jones took it in immense
numbers from a shallow pond on the hill above
Mitcheldean, in the direction of the Wilderness,
of which it appeared to be the only molluscous
inhabitant.

Corbicula consobrina, closely allied to the

Cyclads, inhabits the river Nile, and ranges from thence to Cashmere. It tenanted the estuaries and creeks of Central Europe during the Pleistocene period. It is associated, at Brammerton and Balcham, with extinct species of *Rhinoceros, Hippopotamus, Mastodon,* and *Elephants.* It is also found fossilized with living species of *Cyclas* and *Pisidium,* in the Pleistocene fresh-water marls, at Stutton, Grays, Ilford, and Erith.

CHAPTER III.

WATER-BREATHING SNAILS.

(*Gasteropoda.*)

I.—STRUCTURE AND PHYSIOLOGY OF THE GASTEROPODA.

THE Gasteropods include sea-snails, as the whelk, limpet, &c., and a few fresh-water snails, as the common marsh snail (*Paludina vivipara*), which may be studied as a type of the latter.

Shell. — All the fresh-water snails live in a single or univalve shell, having the form of a more or less conical spiral; it may be regarded as a tube

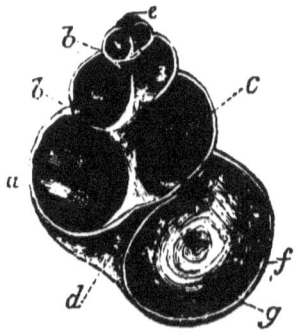

Fig. 4.—Section of the shell of Paludina.

wound upon itself, each turn of which is called a whorl or volution (*a*), fig. 4; the lines of junction of the whorls are called sutures (*b*); by the close coiling of the whorls, a pillar of shell, or *columella* (*c*), in the centre, is left, and such shells are said to be *imperforated;* the axis of the shell, around which the whorls are coiled, is sometimes open or *umbilicated :* this *perforation* may be a mere chink (*d*), or it may be filled by a shelly deposit in the adult, as in many land shells. The last turn of the shell or *body whorl* is usually large. The base of the shell is the end opposite to the apex (*e*); and the *aperture* is *entire* (*f*), that is, not notched or produced into a canal. The margin of the aperture is called the *peristome,* which in *Paludina* is continued all round; in the Rock Snail it becomes so in the adult; more frequently, among the shells of the next class, the *peristome* is *incomplete,* the *left side* of the aperture being formed by the body whorl; the *right side* of the aperture is formed by the *outer lip,* the left side by the *inner,* or *columella lip.* The outer lip is *thin,* not *thickened* or *reflected,* as in the majority of the land shells; but in immature shells of them it is always thin and sharp. The aperture of the shell is upon the right-hand side, when the shell is viewed in a vertical position, with the aperture directed toward you: this is the general rule, but in a few of the shells of the air-breathing snails the shell is twisted in the opposite direction : in the former case the shell is said to be *dextral,* and in the latter, *reversed* or *sinistral.*

Lines of colour or sculpture are termed *spiral* or *longitudinal* when they proceed from the apex around the whorls; *radiating,* if they extend across the whorls; and *transverse* when they coincide with the lines of growth. The shell is secreted by the mantle, and consists of layers of membrane strengthened by calcareous matter, and does not exhibit such an amount of diversity as that of the bivalve shells. The colours which are diffused over the shell are due to the secretion from the mantle, of pigments, which are impregnated chiefly in the epidermal matter.

The aperture of the shell is accurately closed by a horny plate attached to the back of the foot, and is called the *operculum* (*g*); it is calcareous in some other snails. As regards its mode of growth, it is *concentric*, that is, increasing equally all round; in the genus *Valvata* it is *spiral*, growing only on one edge, and revolving as it grows.

Animal.—The body of the animal is enclosed in the mantle, which is open in front, and through which the head and foot project; the abdomen, containing the mass of the viscera, is wound upon itself in the form of the shell. The mantle in its natural position covers the back and forms a large fold or cavity, on the left side of which lie the gills, and into which the terminations of the digestive, reproductive, and urinary organs open. When the snail (see fig. 5) is protruded from its shell, the following parts may be seen:—

The *Foot*, by which it makes its way in the world, is a very broad, flat, expanded disk, and is in close contact with the ventral region of the body; from which circumstance the class has

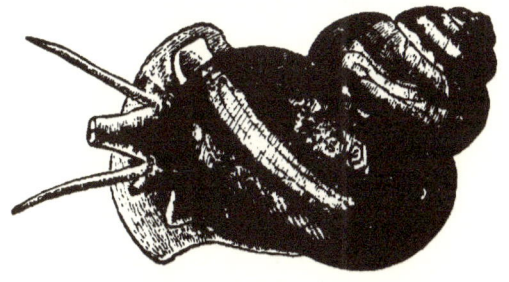

Fig. 5.—*Paludina vivipara* (Woodward).

procured the name " Gasteropoda," or " belly-footed." This organ consists of a mass of inter-woven muscular fibres, and progression is due to the alternate action of a set of muscles on each side.

The *Head* is prolonged into a muzzle, at the extremity of which is the mouth; from the extension of the foot in front, the animal can only feed when at rest. The head bears *two* long and slender *tentacles* or horns with the stalks bearing the eyes attached to them on the outside. The tentacles are extended to the utmost, and are gently swayed to and fro when the snail walks: by means of them the animal feels its way, and is warned of danger. An appendage may be observed on each side of the head arising from the tentacles; that on the right side is the largest. The *operculum* is situated on the hinder part of the foot.

Digestive Organs.—The mouth is armed with an upper horny jaw, and adherent within the cavity is a horny muscular tongue, which is a mechanical organ for the attrition of the food. This *lingual ribbon* or *tongue* (fig. 6, *c*), as it is termed (often, but erroneously, *pallet*), is covered by more or less regular quadrangular plates, carrying erect amber-coloured and glossy teeth of extreme tenuity, which are directed backward. This tongue acts in concert with the horny jaw (*a*), the one holding and the other rasping the vegetable food into the mouth.

As the *lingual ribbon* is such a pretty and interesting object for examination with the microscope, and as it plays so important a part in the economy of all snails and slugs, land, fresh-water, and marine; and also because the teeth vary in number, in arrangement, and in ornamentation in the different genera and species, I will now give a method of preparation, and will also point out, in its proper place, the value in a systematic arrangement of the species of these objects.

The tongue forms the floor of the mouth, and the front part, which is the only part in use, is frequently curved or bent quite over, and its teeth are often broken and blunted; the hinder

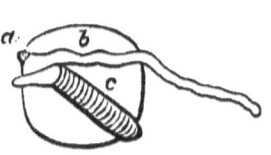

Fig. 6.—Diagrammatic view of the dental apparatus.

portion descends obliquely behind the mouth, and its edges are united to form a tube (*c*), and enclosed in a membranous sheath, which opens gradually as the part is brought forward to replace the worn portion.

The most simple plan to prepare these as microscopic objects is to boil the head of the mollusk in a solution of potash in a test-tube, by which all the parts, with the exception of the tongue and jaw, are dissolved : care must be taken to thoroughly wash the tongue before mounting.

The most instructive method is doubtlessly that of dissection; but certainly, when we have some of our minute snails to deal with, that of maceration will be a great saving of time and patience. The head should be pinned down in a gutta-percha trough containing water enough to cover the part; the floor of the mouth may be laid open by passing the lower point of a pair of scissors into the mouth, and cutting upwards; now pin back the severed portions, and by the aid of a lancet or needle, work out the lingual apparatus. The ribbon should be cleaned by washing with a camel's hair brush, or by soaking in potash-water; if the latter, wash the tongue well before mounting. The preparation may be mounted in *glycerine,* or if intended as an object for the polariscope, it should be mounted in Canada balsam.

E

The length of the lingual ribbon is short in *Paludina,* but is of varying length for different species; in the marine limpet it is longer than the whole animal. The teeth are distributed in straight longitudinal rows, and in transverse rows, which are variously curved, angular, or rarely straight. The number of the teeth in the transverse row is nearly constant for the same species, and the number of rows is exceedingly variable in different species; longitudinally the teeth are usually arranged in a triple series, and each transverse row is but a repetition of the rest. The central area is called the *rachis,* and the teeth form usually a single series; the lateral areas are called the *pleuræ,* the teeth on which are termed *uncini,* and usually are extremely numerous. The term *laterals* is employed in a restricted sense to designate a series of teeth intermediate between the *rachidian* and the *uncini.*

The lingual ribbon of *Paludina vivipara* con-

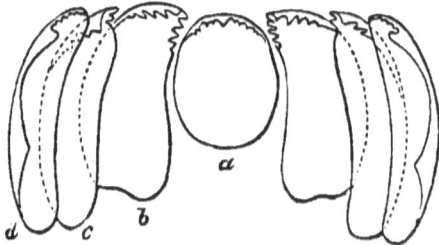

Fig. 7.—Teeth of *Paludina vivipara* (Lovèn).

sists of a few transverse rows, each composed of

a central oval tooth (*a*), slightly hooked and denticulated; and three nearly similar *uncini* (*b*, *c*, *d*), which are oblong and toothed on the upper sides: the number of teeth in each transverse row is therefore seven.

The number and arrangement of the teeth are capable of easy representation by a numerical formula. Thus, 3. 1. 3 represents the system in *Paludina*, signifying that each transverse row consists of one *median* or *rachidian* tooth, flanked on each side by three *uncini*.

In *Vitrina* the general formula is ∞. 1. ∞; where ∞ represents 37; and as there are 100 rows, the lingual teeth of *Vitrina* are 7,500; the formula will now stand $\frac{37 \cdot 1 \cdot 37}{100} = 7,500$. In the great slug, *Limax maximus*, there are 28,800 teeth, distributed in 160 rows of 180 teeth in each. The number of teeth has no relation to the size of the animal; thus, *Helicella cellaria* possesses 1,330, while *H. nitidula*, less in size, has nearly three times that number.

The above dental formula will be employed to indicate the number of teeth in each generic group or species, as the case may be.

The teeth of the fresh-water Gasteropods are characterized by their fewness, whilst those of air-breathing snails are remarkable for their extraordinary number.

The digestive apparatus further consists of a

long gullet (fig. 6, *b*), an intestinal canal, folded in the substance of the liver, bent to the right, and terminating close to the margin of the mantle in about the middle line of the body. The liver occupies a very large part of the abdomen.

The *Circulatory System* is somewhat more perfect than in the bivalves.

The *Respiration* is aquatic; the organ is a plume-like gill, formed of a series of triangular plates attached to the left side of the branchial cavity. The water passes into this chamber through a respiratory siphon formed by the folding of a small lappet of the neck.

The *Nervous System* is much the same as in the bivalves. The *eyes* are two in number, placed on short stalks attached to the conical tentacles. The *organs of hearing* are situated near the base of the tentacles, and are sacs containing an otolith suspended in a fluid. The sense of smell is possessed by Gasteropods, and that of touch in a high degree; the tentacles are endowed with great sensitiveness.

Reproduction. — The sexes are distinct in *Paludina* ; the eggs are retained within the oviduct of the parent until they are hatched, and the young are not excluded until they have attained a considerable growth. *Paludina* is therefore *ovoviviparous.* The young are at first exceedingly unlike the parent; they are provided with a delicate nautilus-like shell, and closed by an operculum; on each side of the head there extends a fin-like membrane, the edges of which are fringed with cilia, by means of which they swim within the contents of the egg. In most of the oviparous snails, on the rupture of the egg-cases, the young swim forth with great activity by the action of the lobes, and are dispersed far and wide.

Habits, Food, &c.—*Paludina* is a sluggish animal; it feeds on vegetable matter, and prefers nearly stagnant waters, or very slow-running rivers with a bottom of soft mud; it buries itself for weeks in the mud, and crawls up at intervals.

II.—DESCRIPTION OF THE SPECIES.

The fresh-water Gasteropods of Great Britain are grouped in the families *Paludinidæ, Littorinidæ,* and *Neritinidæ.*

FAMILY PALUDINIDÆ (*Marsh Shells*).

This family contains a few genera of fresh-water snails distributed in all parts of the world. In Great Britain three generic groups occur: *Paludina,* the type of the family; *Bithinia,* and *Valvata*. *Paludina* is ovoviviparous, *Bithinia* and *Valvata* are oviparous; the operculum of *Paludina* and *Valvata* is horny, of *Bithinia* shelly. *Valvata* is distinguished from the others by the presence of a long plume-like gill, which is partially protruded when the animal is crawling, and by the more circular whorls composing the shell.

The lingual ribbon of *Paludinidæ* is very simple, and presents the same general features throughout the family, and places it in close proximity to the periwinkles and others comprised in the family *Littorinidæ*.

The general formula is 3.1.3; the number of transverse rows is very limited.

Genus Paludina.

PALUDINA VIVIPARA—(*the Common Marsh Shell*) (Pl. IV., fig. 26).—The specific name *vivipara* was given to this species by Linnæus, from the animal being ovoviviparous, that is to say, the eggs are retained within the interior of the parent until they are hatched; it is a peculiarity possessed by other species of the genus. As the next species very closely resembles the present one, it will be necessary to give a full description of it.

The shell is conically oval, rather solid, of rather dull yellowish-green, with three broad

Plate IV.

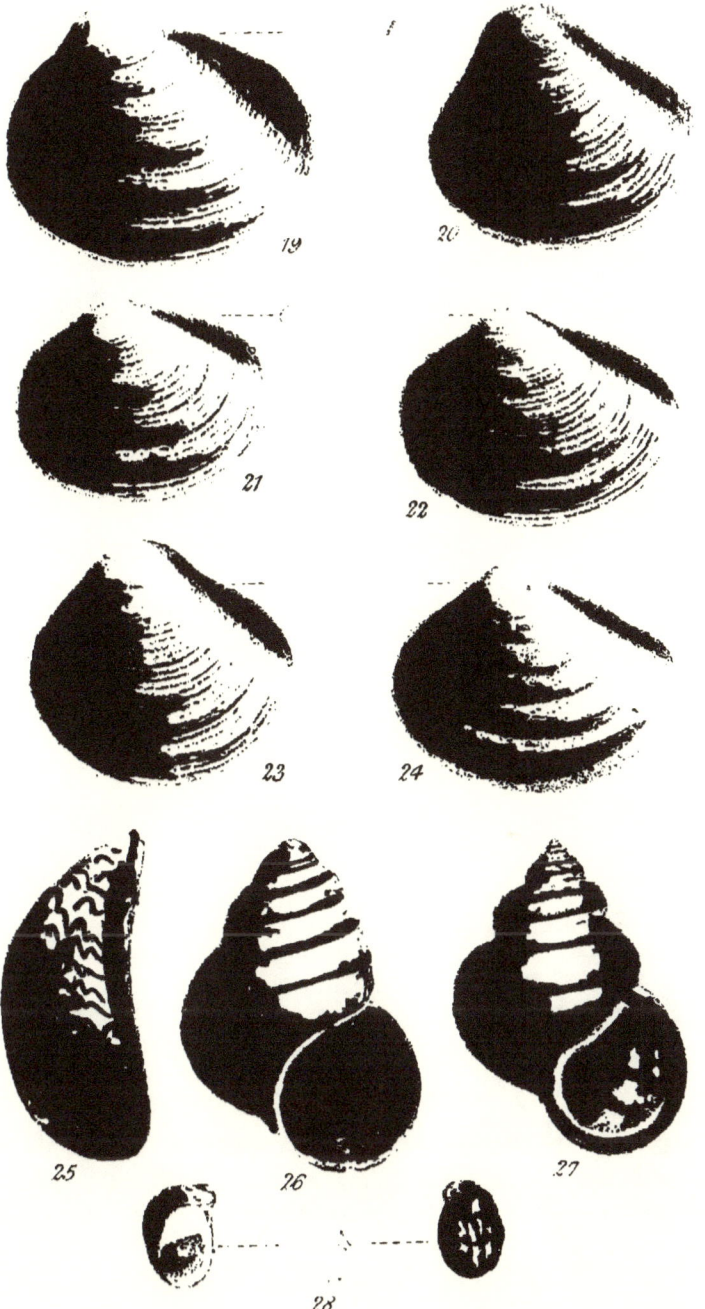

Vincent Brooks, Imp

brown spiral bands on the last whorl, and two upon each of the two preceding whorls ; the shell is also finely striated longitudinally; whorls six, rather convex, with a well-defined suture; aperture oval, peristome continuous, umbilicus represented by a narrow slit behind the inner lip ; the operculum horny, rather thick. Length an inch and a half, and one inch broad. The body is a dark grey, or brown speckled with yellow. The young shells are sometimes, at least, clothed with a downy epidermis, rising into short spines round the middle of each whorl,—disappearing much on dying.

In the timber docks on the Thames, and in the various canals about London, this species is very abundant, and in fine condition. Following the ramifications of our system of water-roads, the species inhabits the Kent and Avon canals, the canals of Gloucestershire, Staffordshire, &c. ; but is by no means restricted to such habitats, for it is found in many of the slow rivers in the midland and southern counties of England. It occurs in the river Ouse and Barnsley Canal, at Wakefield, in Yorkshire, which are probably its northern limits. Dead shells of this species and of some southern forms are frequently introduced with the ballast into localities where it is not indigenous.

M. Joly, after keeping several individuals of

Paludina vivipara without food for three months, submitted them in their enfeebled state to a temperature of 23° F., and on dissolving their icy prisons he found them all living.   He in a like manner experimented with *Anodon cygneus* with similar results.

PALUDINA LISTERI (Pl. IV., fig. 27) differs from *P. vivipara* in its shell being thinner and shorter, the whorls more inflated or swollen, and the sutures consequently deeper, the mouth more circular, and the umbilicus more distinct.   It is usually somewhat larger.

This species is generally associated with the last, but is not of such frequent occurrence.

The shells of this species collected from a pond on Hampstead Heath, London, have their apices eroded, which is due to the action of sulphuretted hydrogen given off from the decomposing animal and vegetable matters.

The animal is very sluggish, and on being touched generally falls off the body upon which it may be crawling.   The female in the autumn contains from twenty to thirty eggs, and the young are excluded at the end of two months.

Genus Bithinia.

BITHINIA TENTACULATA—(*the Tentacled Bithinia*) (Pl. III., fig. 14)—is a very common species on aquatic plants in streams, ditches, and canals throughout Great Britain. The shell is ovately conical, of a yellowish horn-colour, smooth and semi-transparent, very frequently incrusted with a green confervoid growth. There are five or six whorls, the last one large; aperture oval, angular behind, the shelly operculum closely fitting the aperture, no umbilicus. Shell half-inch long, three-tenths wide. The animal is blackish, speckled with golden-yellow dots; the foot is lobed in front, narrow and rounded behind; the tentacles long and slender; eyes black, large, and sessile. Bouchard says that Bithinias deposit their eggs on stones and aquatic plants; the female lays from thirty to seventy eggs in a band of three rows, cleaning the surface as she proceeds; the young are hatched in three or four weeks, and attain their full growth in the second year.

BITHINIA LEACHII (Pl. III., fig. 13), named after Dr. Leach, one of the earliest systematic writers on English zoology. The shell of this species is much smaller than that of the last, being about a quarter of an inch long and two lines broad; the whorls are more swollen and rounded, distinctly separated by a deep suture; the aperture is nearly circular, and there is a small umbilicus. It is found in the same habitats as the last, but is local and less abundant, and is confined more to the southern and middle counties of England.

It can live in slightly brackish waters under tidal influence, as along the banks of the Thames below London.   Dr. Gray says that the eggs are disposed on a tough strap-shaped green membrane, in a double row, consisting of six or seven pairs; the whole is fixed to the under side of aquatic plants.

GENUS VALVATA.

VALVATA PISCINALIS—(*the Stream Valve-shell*) (Pl. II., fig. 5), so named from inhabiting fishponds. The shell of this species is readily distinguished; it is globular, of four rounded well-defined whorls; colour brownish-yellow, very finely ridged, in a spiral direction; aperture circular, united all round, with a thin greyish-white operculum; there is a deep central umbilicus.   Length one-fourth of an inch, and as much broad.   The shell is very variable in the degree of elevation of the spire, and consequently in its diameter relatively to its height.   The lingual ribbon of

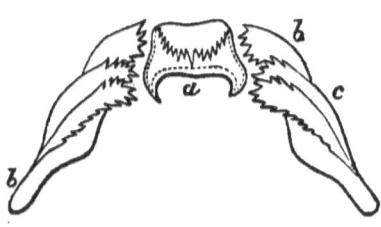

Fig. 8.—Teeth of *V. piscinalis* (Lovèn).

V. piscinalis is long; the central tooth (*a*, fig. 8) is subquadrate, with a produced base; hooked and denticulated; the three *uncini* (*b*, *c*, *b*) are lanceolate, and toothed on each side.   A common

and widely-distributed species, very abundant
on the bottoms of shallow muddy streams, on
marsh lands, or on aquatic plants in ditches and
canals.

Mr. Benson some years since favoured me
with what appeared to be a shell of this species;
but, strange to say, it was the house of a South
American species of caddis-worm. The domicile
was a perfect imitation of the shell of our little
V. piscinalis, and of the same size. The mate-
rials of which it is constructed are not the less
singular. The spiral valvata-like tube was of
the ordinary secreted matter, to which were
affixed remarkably fine grains of sand; and for
an operculum the scale of a fish was ingeniously
appropriated.

VALVATA CRISTATA—(*the Crested Valve-shell*)
(Pl. II., fig. 6)—is a minute species, living on
the aquatic vegetation of lakes, ponds, canals,
and ditches; and though it is widely diffused
throughout our islands, is by no means a
common species. The shell is flat, like that
of a *Planorbis,* but easily distinguished from
it by the continuous margin of the aperture, being circular, like that of *V. piscinalis,*
for which it could never be mistaken; for in all
stages of growth the shell of this species is flat
above, whereas that of *V. piscinalis* is more or
less globular. The shell is only one-tenth of an

inch in diameter, and is of a pale horn-colour, finely striated transversely, with three whorls.

The animal of this handsomely-formed species (Pl. XI., fig. 143), like that of *V. piscinalis*, has a plume-like gill, furnished with about fifteen branches on each side, which is usually partially protruded on the right side when the animal is crawling; on the same side of the animal there is an accessory respiratory organ, in the form of a filament, arising from the mantle: in the present species this appendage is rather shorter than the tentacles, which it so much resembles; its position, however, will not allow us to regard it as one.

FAMILY NERITIDÆ.

GENUS NERITINA, *diminutive of Nerita, a sea-snail.*

NERITINA FLUVIATILIS — (*the River Neritine*) (Pl. IV., fig. 28)—is the only British representative of the large family *Neritidæ* of tropical seas and rivers, characterized by a thick semiglobular shell. The species of *Neritina* are more especially confined to rivers, and have small globular shells, coloured by bands or spots, and furnished with shelly opercula. The pretty speckled species found abundantly in many of the English rivers adhering to stones and to other shells, is about three-eighths of an inch long, by a quarter broad, composed of three whorls, the last one excessively disproportionate; the spire very short, and as if lateral. A polished brownish-green horny epidermis covers the shell; in dead shells the beautiful spots or bands of white purplish-brown or pale brown are seen to perfection, for in fresh shells this colouring is much hidden by the epidermis, but may be seen by the aid of a magnifying-glass.

The species is common in all the larger rivers where the bottom is stony, and in canals upon stones. It does not occur in the north of Ireland, and is rare in Scotland, but is recorded from Loch Stennis, in the Orkneys.

The animal is rarely to be seen in motion : it crawls slowly, with the shell slightly raised; the long, slender divergent tentacles, the large black eyes, placed on short stalks at the base of the tentacles, are then shown; the skin is covered with stiff silky hairs.

The lingual teeth (see fig. 9) :—the central tooth (*a*) is minute; the first lateral tooth is

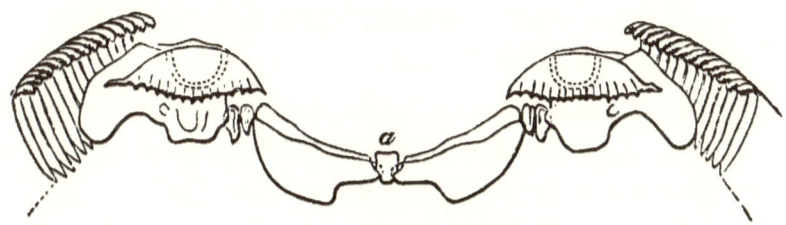

Fig. 9.—Teeth of *Neritina fluviatilis* (Lovèn).

large, subtriangular, succeeded by two very minute ones; the *uncini* are about sixty in number; the first one is very large, and of a remarkable shape; the rest are very slender, hooked, and denticulated.

Each female deposits her egg-capsules in clusters of fifty or sixty, on the surface of the shell of her neighbour and not to her own; sometimes, but rarely, to stones, or to the shells of other mollusks. Each capsule contains from forty to sixty eggs, but only one embryo is developed; for the other eggs constitute the food of the young *Neritina* until it quits the capsule. The capsules, which are usually mistaken for the eggs, are globular, and consist of two separable portions; the upper and larger falls off when the young is about to escape; the lower portion remains attached to the surface of the foster-parent's shell, the raised margins of which produce small indentations.—*Claperède.*

The young appear in August and September, and creep about on the shells or stones which bore their egg-capsules, feeding on the microscopic organisms, diatoms, algæ, &c., which now serve for its nourishment.

Family Littorinidæ.

The three following species have little claim to be regarded as fresh-water shells; the above family, to which they belong, contains the periwinkles and numerous other marine snails. The family may be distinguished from the preceding ones by the shell being spiral and conical, the operculum spiral, and the eyes sessile at the outer bases of the tentacles.

The genus ASSIMINIA (from the Latin *assimilis*, very like) is represented by one British species, ASSIMINIA GRAYANA (Pl. II., fig. 8), inhabiting the banks of the river Thames between Greenwich and Gravesend, living on the mud beneath the shade afforded by *Scirpus maritimus, Festuca arundinacea*, &c. It is very abundant.

The animal of *Assiminia* differs from the marine *Rissoa*, in the tentacles being united to the eye-stalks, which equal them in length. The shell of *A. Grayana* is ovate, acute, solid, shining, of a liver-brown colour, and is about

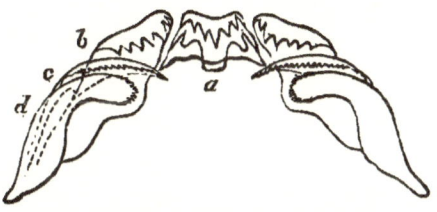

Fig. 10.—Teeth of *A. Grayana* (Lovèn).

a quarter of an inch in length; the whorls are five in number; the suture is slightly impressed; there is no umbilicus; the aperture is ovate; the operculum is horny, ovate, and of a

black-brown colour. The teeth are seven in
number; the central with a base produced
into a horn, with five to seven pointed lobes;
the first lateral tooth with seven lobes; the
second is slender, claw-like, and serrated; the
third is rounded at the tip, with minute denticulations.—*Lovèn*.

In company with the last species are two other
brackish-water shells, belonging to the allied
genus HYDROBIA, species of which are more particularly marine. *Hydrobia* differs from *Assiminia*
in having the eyes placed on tubercles, and from
Rissoa in its smooth shell.

The form of the shell of one species, HYDROBIA
SIMILIS (Pl. II., fig. 7), resembles that of *Bithinia
Leachii*, but is distinguished by its smaller size
and grooved suture; the operculum is horny,
concentric, with the nucleus lateral; whereas in
Bithinia it is somewhat shelly, and marked by
concentric ridges having the nucleus central.

A second species, HYDROBIA VENTROSA, is
closely allied to *H. ulvæ*, whose habits are more
marine, from which it differs in being half the
size, with a deeper suture; from *H. similis* in its
longer spire, and the absence of the channelled
suture, and by its much smaller umbilicus. This
latter species is very abundant on many parts of
our coasts, in estuaries and in brackish water, or
upon the mud banks of tidal rivers.

CHAPTER IV.

AIR-BREATHING SNAILS.

CLASS PULMONIFERA.

THIS class embraces all the land snails, land slugs, and such of the water snails which breathe air : they are closely related to *Paludina*, and to the plant-eating sea snails. Their breathing organ is the simplest form of lung, formed by the folding of the mantle, over which the blood-vessels are distributed, and occupies the same position as the branchial chamber of *Paludina*, &c. This chamber opens externally by a round contractile aperture on the margin of the mantle over the neck, on the right side. There is no special mechanism of respiration. The functions of both sexes are united in each individual. The Pulmonifera vary much in appearance and habits. The form and number of teeth on the lingual ribbon' afford good characters for the distinction of genera and families, as also for the separation of allied species. The class is divided into two orders,—*Inoperculata*, without an operculum, and *Operculata*, possessing an operculum.

F

The INOPERCULATA, or typical Pulmonifera, are naturally divided into the slugs, land snails, and water snails; and are embraced in the following families :—

1. { Animal slug-like 2
   {   ,,   contained in a more or less spiral shell ... 3

2. { Mantle small, shield-like ... ... *Limacidæ*
   {   ,,   enveloping the body... ... ... *Oncidiadæ*

3. { Two pairs of retractile tentacles ... ... *Heliculæ*
   { Tentacles two, eyes sessile 4

4. { Animal aquatic, aperture of shell edentulous, *Limnæidæ*
   { Aperture of shell toothed ... ... *Auriculidæ*

SLUGS (FAMILY LIMACIDÆ).

Slugs are very conspicuous among the mollusca, and readily recognized by their elongated, more or less naked bodies. The body is united in its whole length with the foot beneath; the head is furnished with four cylindrical tentacles, and eyes are situated on the upper pair. The slugs resemble in many respects the snails, and are regarded by the vulgar as such, which have the peculiar power of leaving their shells during the summer and retiring to them again for protection on the approach of winter; so that, if this were true, we ought only to find snails during one season and slugs during another. But the snail cannot leave its shell, being attached to it by muscles. There are many points of difference between these two familiar animals. Firstly, one afforded by the nature and position of the shell. Observe the oval prominence on the back of that large spotted slug (*Limax maximus*) ; this is the mantle which in the snail forms a sack through which the head and foot protrude, but in the slug covers but a small part of the body. Beneath the shield-like mantle lies a thin shelly plate which protects the viscera. A snail may be viewed in the light of a slug whose visceral matter and mantle are elongated upwards, and then spirally coiled, the mantle secreting an external shell, instead of depositing shelly matter from its inner surface. The shelly plate of the slugs has been called the snail's stone, and was formerly esteemed a valuable medicine in cases of gravel and strangury. This internal shell varies in size, structure, and position in the different species and genera, a fact overlooked by Swammerdam ; for to account for large slugs having "very small membranous plates, while the smaller ones had them often much larger, and formed of solid stone," he was inclined to think "that the snails change this their little stone yearly, in the same manner as crawfish change those two semiconvex and plain stones which are likewise placed in their thorax, and are improperly called crab's eyes." Beneath the mantle on the right side of the

F 2

body is an aperture leading into the respiratory orifice.

The lingual ribbon of the slugs is characterized by its numerous transverse rows, containing a large number of very similar teeth; in general, the central tooth has a long central point with a small denticulation on each side of it; the lateral teeth, as they approach the margin, become spine-like, having but a long projecting point.

All molluscous animals excrete a mucous fluid to lubricate the skin, furnished by glands situated in it; the slugs copiously exude this slime, more especially when irritated. The "silvery slimy trails" of slugs and snails are depositions of mucus left in their tracks. The slugs are divided into four genera, characterized principally by the relative positions of the mantle, shell, and respiratory orifice. Thus in *Arion* the shell is represented by mere calcareous granules in the mantle; the respiratory orifice is near the fore part of the shield; the body is truncated behind, and terminated by a mucous gland. In *Limax* the shell is of the nature of a thin oblong, or slightly concave plate, the mantle-shield marked with concentric lines, and the respiratory orifice near the hind part of the shield. *Geomalacus* has a gland at the extremity of the tail like *Arion*, the respiratory orifice nearer the front than in *Limax*, and the internal shell claw-shaped. In *Testacella* we have a near approach to the snails, and through *Vitrina* is connected with them; the shell is small, ear-shaped, placed externally at the hinder extremity of the body, and covers the mantle, beneath which, on the right side, is the respiratory orifice.

GENUS ARION.

Arion was a horse remarkable for its speed, but our *Arion* is remarkably slow.

ARION ATER—(*the Black Slug*) (Pl. V., fig. 31)— is familiar to all as a common object of our gardens and waysides, and is also too well known to the gardener, as being more or less injurious to the early cabbages and other garden produce; and in the autumn as one among other mollusks that mutilate and render repulsive the fruits of that season. Dead animal matter—even that of their own species—does not come amiss to them; they also feed on the common earthworm.

The adult animal is usually brownish or greyish-black; at other times brown or reddish; the young individuals are grey, whitish, bluish-white, or yellow-coloured. It attains a length of from three to five inches. The shell is composed of loosely aggregated calcareous particles.

Cuvier writes, that "the finest injections do not produce anything more agreeable to the eye of the anatomist than the white ramifications of the arteries in the black slug." The arteries are opaque and milk-white, and strongly contrast with the dark grounds upon which they trace their course; as, for example, the dark green of the intestines, or the blackish-brown of the liver. The heart is included in a very thin bag, or *pericardium*, in the cavity of which there is abundance of a watery fluid, as clear as crystal.

Arion ater frequents damp and shady woods and thickets, gardens, and hedge-banks; during the day it is never seen abroad, except after rain, retiring under stones and logs of timber, or burying itself in the earth; for the dry atmosphere would deprive the body of its moisture, so essential to the existence of the animal.

It deposits its globular, semi-transparent eggs in May, among the roots of plants. This slug, as also some other of the larger species, is infested by a small yellowish-white mite, *Philodromus limacum* of Jenyns, who has given a very interesting account of the habits of the little animal. The parasites may be seen running in some numbers over the body of the slug. It is curious that the slimy surface of the slug's back does not impede the progress of these mites ; but they seem never to be at rest, moving with the greatest rapidity. A striking feature in the history of the little animal is that it appears to take up its abode within the interior of the slug ; effecting an entry by means of the respiratory aperture, and coming forth occasionally to ramble over the surface of the body. The slug does not appear to suffer any inconvenience from these parasites, and even allows them to run in and out of the lateral orifice without betraying the slightest symptoms of irritation. *Arion ater* has a wide geographical range.

ARION HORTENSIS—(*the Garden Arion Slug*) (Pl. V., fig. 29)—differs from the last species ; it is much smaller and more slender, and is provided with grey longitudinal stripes. The foot is bordered with orange. The imperfect shell is more compact than that of *A. ater*.

The horny jaw (fig. 11) is arched, strongly ribbed, and its margin crenulated ; it contrasts strongly with the smooth rostrated jaw of *Limax* (see fig. 12).

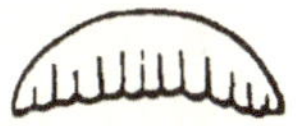

Fig. 11.—Jaw of *A. hortensis.*

Like the last species, it is common in woods, damp hedges, and gardens. The eggs of this species are said to be phosphorescent for the first fifteen days after they have been laid.

GENUS LIMAX (*Limax*, a slug).

The *Limaces* differ little from the *Arions*, but are destitute of a mucous pore at the end of the tail; the mantle is concentrically marked and not granulated, and the respiratory aperture near the hind part of its border; the tail is carinated, or ridged.

The horny jaw of *Limax* (fig. 12) is strongly

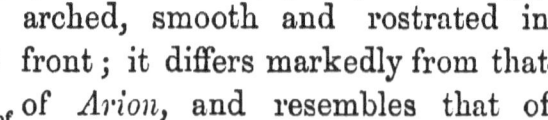

arched, smooth and rostrated in front; it differs markedly from that of *Arion*, and resembles that of *Helicella* (fig. 18) and *Vitrina*.

Fig. 12.—Jaw of *L. gagates.*

The species feed chiefly on tender herbage, fruits, and vegetable substances in general; they are very voracious, feeding after rain, or in the evening to early morn; during the heat of the day they remain concealed, and during droughts and frosts they are torpid, buried underground. They are the great pests of our gardens and cultivated lands,—to young oats, peas, tares, clover, and turnips, they give preference; and many fields have been made barren by them, and have had to be ploughed down and resown. Although vegetables are the legitimate food of the slug, most of them are occasionally carnivorous, not from necessity, but from pure and decisive choice; some of them may be even convicted of cannibalism. They have, however,

Plate V

29

30

31

32

33

34

35

numerous enemies, especially among birds : the principal of these are the blackbird and thrush,

> —— whose notes
> Nice finger'd Art must emulate in vain.

Ducks and geese are very partial to slugs.

The *Limaces* when irritated withdraw their heads beneath the mantle ; this attitude is also assumed during repose.

LIMAX MAXIMUS (Pl. V., fig. 32), so called from its being the largest of the slugs, attains the length of five or six inches. This large grey slug is spotted and striped with black. The shell is thin, flat, oblong, about six lines long and four broad. The dental formula is $\frac{90 \cdot 1 \cdot 90}{160}$.

This species is widely distributed, is a frequent visitor to our pantries and cellars, lurking in damp corners, or remaining concealed in the dust-bins, or other sheltered situations, during the day ; foraging during the night, its perambulations are rendered distinctly visible by its trail, for the thick glutinous slime which is copiously exuded becomes very iridescent when dry. It is very omnivorous, preferring certainly, as indicated by its attachment to the dwellings of man, the refuse from our kitchens and the delicacies of our tables when within its reach. It is, however, frequent in moist woods, hybernating in the mossy crevices of trees, or in decaying wood, or enveloping itself in dead leaves in damp situations.

The eggs are white, and are deposited in a cluster under stones in spring. Like *Arion ater*, this *Limax* is infested with the slug-mite.

LIMAX FLAVUS — (*the Yellow Slug*) (Pl. VI., fig. 39).—This slug has a yellowish body, spotted with blackish-brown, and with numerous undulated or granulated ridges. The dental formula is $\frac{61 \cdot 1 \cdot 61}{166}$. The shield is short, broadly rounded behind, and marked with concentric granulated wrinkles. The shell is thin, very like that of *L. maximus*, but is smaller, about four lines long, and two and a half broad. It differs from *L. maximus* in having the end of the tail keeled, and in its inferior size and different markings. This large fleshy slug attains the length of four or five inches.

Its slime is limpid and yellow, but when the animal is irritated it secretes a thick bluish-white mucus.

The species is gregarious and active, and is commonly found in cellars and damp places in our large towns. At nightfall it sallies forth from its place of retreat to feast upon the refuse lying about; it cleans bones well, and is fond of boiled potatoes and table delicacies: they invariably retire to their quarters at the approach of morning. When a candle-light is brought near them they shrink back, but for a moment, and leisurely pursue their way; by the aid of this light they are pretty objects in their almost transparent flesh variegated with markings. It also occurs in damp places, beneath stones, and among plants in woods.

L. flavus is one of the few European Pulmonifera introduced to America; it occurs rarely in Portland, Maine.

LIMAX AGRESTIS—(*the Field Slug*) (Pl. V., fig. 30).—The form is oblong, very convex above, the shield large, broader behind, marked with concentric lines; the body on the upper side of a yellowish-grey or pale brownish-yellow, often mottled with dusky and whitish, with numerous longitudinal interrupted ridges; it varies considerably in colour, being sometimes whitish or cream-coloured, or grey or dusky; back with a short keel, bent obliquely towards the end; the under side pale grey, margined with yellow. Length about an inch and a half; shell one line and a half long and one broad, concave above, concentrically wrinkled, with a membranaceous margin. The horny jaw is crescent-shaped, with blunt ends; the exterior surface is marked with numerous slight longitudinal ribs, which project over the cutting edge; the dental formula is $\frac{32 \cdot 1 \cdot 32}{100}$, the central plate is longer than wide, carrying a tooth as long as itself, shouldered at the base;

the laterals similar, but the apex not so central; the uncini are bidentated.

It is abundant, and generally distributed in fields, gardens, and woods. In gardens it is a serious pest; its ravages among crops, as oats, peas, clover, and tares, are such as often to necessitate the resowing of the land. We give a recipe for a decoy for snails and slugs:—Warm cabbage leaves until they are quite soft; suffuse the hands slightly with unsalted greasy matter, pass the leaves one by one between the hands, so that some taint of grease may be transferred to the leaf. Lay the leaves in the haunts of the slugs, which will attract them to their destruction. A few ducks, however, will be found to relieve one's garden of these pests more effectually than such agencies.

Limax agrestis is unfortunately very prolific, producing several families in the course of a year; according to M. Bouchard, two individuals have been observed to lay no fewer than 380 eggs. A very subtle enemy is at work at a very early period of the slug's life; for M. Laurent has found a fungus in the eggs, even before they are excluded from the parent.

The field slug is somewhat carnivorous, and cannibal-like inclined. When irritated, it emits a thick milky slime, which, when dry, leaves a white film: the nature of this slime and the small size of the animal serve to distinguish this species.

L. agrestis is common in fields, and abundant in cellars and gardens in Portland, Maine; it is indigenous to Greenland.

LIMAX BRUNNEUS—(*the Brown Slug*) (Pl. VI., fig. 42).—This slug was added to the British fauna by the late Dr. Johnston, of Berwick, who observed that it differed from every variety of *Limax agrestis* in its darker colour, its colourless mucus, in the abrupt termination of the tail, in the position of the shield, which is nearly central when the animal is fully extended, and in the size of the shield, which is as long as the posterior half of the body; nor is there any keel on this part.

It inhabits shady woods, in damp places, under stones, and amongst decaying leaves; and is comparatively rare in Berwickshire and in the north-east of England; at Thirsk, Yorkshire; woods between Cooper's Hill and Birdlip, Gloucester (*Jones*).

LIMAX TENELLUS—(*the Tender Slug*) (Pl. V., fig. 34).—This species finds a place in the list of British slugs in that a single specimen was found in a wood at Allansford, in Northumberland. The animal is yellow, with the back rounded, compressed near the tail; shield wrinkled; mucus yellow.

LIMAX ARBORUM—(*the Tree Slug*) (Pl. V., fig. 33).—This arboreal species bears a considerable resemblance to the young of *L. maximus*, from which it may be distinguished by the upper tentacles being much shorter, in proportion, than those of that species, and in the less pointed hinder margin of the shield. In colour it is greyish, spotted with yellowish-white, with a central dusky stripe and a darker band on each side. The back rounded, carinated at the tail; the shield wrinkled, and pointed behind; upper tentacles short. The length of the body nearly three inches. The shell is oval, thin, nearly flat.

This species is not well known, and its apparent rarity is due to its being mistaken for the young of *L. maximus*. Its habitats are, however, not those of that species. It lives on trees, especially the beech, and those that are decaying, feeding on the wood. It also may be found under stones, and under fallen trunks in woods, or even upon bare rocks. Like some other slugs, the young descend from the branches of the trees by threads of slime. This species has been met with throughout Great Britain by several critical observers, though generally absent from local lists of species.

The capability of this species of letting itself down from a height to the ground by the tenacity of the slime exuded from the body, is a feat that most slugs can perform. Certainly the other species, as *L. agrestis*, *L. Sowerbii*, &c., do not appear to possess the same facility, and are more reluctant in resorting to this expedient for escaping from places they have no liking for; they, however, may be forced to use this means for conveying themselves in safety to the ground by leaving them on an evergreen or other tree which may not be congenial to their tastes, when they will speedily effect their escape in this manner.

The thread spun by *L. arborum* is not stouter than a cobweb, and is of a uniform thickness, except close to the body, where it is sensibly thicker. The slug can climb up its suspended thread; in doing which, the head is curved upwards and inwards until it touches the hinder portion of the body; the animal then takes the thread and advances with great facility.

It has been observed at Sandown, Isle of Wight; Connor cliffs, Dingle; Nottingham, preferring walnut trees; Thirsk, at an elevation of 900 feet; Gloucestershire.

LIMAX SOWERBII—(*the Keeled Slug*) (Pl. V., fig. 35).—This and the following species are readily distinguished among the Limaces, by the back being keeled throughout its whole length, and by the finely granulated shield.

The colour of *L. Sowerbii* is yellowish, speckled with brown; head and horns black; shield as if minutely warted with a furrow near its margin. Shell oval, thickened, two or three lines long, and one and a half to two broad.

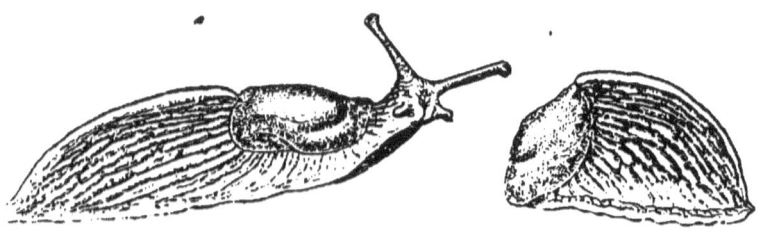

Fig. 13.—*Limax Sowerbii.*

The keeled slug, when at its greatest extension, is about three inches in length; its graceful and lanceolate figure, neat yellowish-brown hue, and the amber-coloured keel, make it really not such a disagreeable object for a slug. The hinder portion of the body is much compressed; the shield measures three-quarters of an inch. When touched, it withdraws the head under the mantle, and contracts to about an inch and a half in length, as in fig. 13. In drought they exhibit greater contractedness, and the smaller specimens when covered with particles of soil and dust, resemble so many pellets of mould. The keel is folded into transverse wrinkles on the contraction of the animal. The dental formula is $\frac{50.1.50}{80}$.

L. Sowerbii is common in gardens and shady places in the vicinity of most of the cities and towns of the South; Sandown, Isle of Wight; Norwich; Chester; becoming rare northwards. In Ireland, Cork, Dublin, Youghal, and Galway. It occurs in the South of France and in Spain.

They feed on cabbages and other vegetables, when in a more or less decayed condition, are very destructive to the celery and bulbs under ground. They are foul feeders, and, like other slugs, have a decided liking to animal matter, devouring the dead remains of each other, and not refusing carrion: they have been observed feeding on living smaller ones of their own species.

They lay their eggs in clusters of about a dozen, in the soil, towards the end of the year. The eggs are oval, soft, elastic, two-tenths of an inch and more in breadth, transparent.

They are infested with *Philodromus limacum.*

Limax gagates—(*the Jet-black Slug*) (Pl. VI., fig. 36)—is a local species; it is found in several localities in Ireland; plentiful near S. Shields; rare in the South of England; Sandown, Isle of Wight; Tenby; and the Isle of Cumbra, Clyde. It resembles *L. Sowerbii* in the back being keeled or carinated throughout, and in its granulated shield; it differs from it in colour, and in the

relative proportion of the shield and body.   Its
general colour is lead-grey, tawny, dark red, or
even black, becoming paler towards the sides, and
near the margin of the foot almost white.   The
shield, usually of a darker colour than the body,
is oblong, rounded behind, and somewhat truncate in front, much larger than in *L. Sowerbii*.
The respiratory orifice is placed nearer the centre
than in that species.   When at rest, the strongly
carinated back is beautifully arched ; it then assumes a more rounded form than any other slug, its
height scarcely exceeding its length.   It is more
than two inches in length when in motion.   The
slime is colourless, thick, and glutinous.   The
eggs are transparent and globular, and appear
to be deposited during the winter, or at the close
of the autumn.   It is a shy and retiring species,
seldom venturing from its retreat in dusk or
during dull weather.   Like the others of its race,
it is very pernicious and destructive to tender
plants.

Limax gagates is a littoral animal ; in Great
Britain it is attached to the neighbourhood of
the sea.   On the continent, from the department
of Finisterre, in France, it follows the sea borders
of Morbihan, Charente-Inférieure, Gironde, &c.,
passes into Spain and Portugal, and appears on
the shores of the Mediterranean in many places
in Italy, Sicily, Algeria, Morocco, &c.

Genus Geomalacus.

GEOMALACUS MACULOSUS—(*the Spotted Irish Slug*) (Pl. VI., fig. 40)—was discovered by Mr. W. Andrews, in 1842, in co. Kerry. This interesting slug-like mollusk is generically allied to *Arion*, and is a remarkable link between it and *Limax*. It differs from both in the position of the generative aperture; its shell approaches to that of *Limax*, is solid, flat, unguiform; the respiratory orifice is placed more anteriorly than in *Limax*; and it possesses a mucous gland at the extremity of the tail. *G. maculosus* is an exceedingly beautiful animal; its length when creeping is about two inches; the colour of the whole upper surface is black, elegantly spotted with yellow or white; the under surface of the foot light-yellow, and divided into three nearly equal bands; the margin of the foot is brown, transversely furrowed. Dr. Allman describes it as possessing a singular power of elongating itself so as at times to assume the appearance of a worm; by this means it can insinuate itself into apertures which we could scarcely conceive it possible for it to enter.

The haunts of *Geomalacus* are thus depicted by its discoverer :—

" Lake Carogh lies to the south of Castlemain

Bay, in the county of Kerry, and stretches nearly north and south five miles. The lake narrows at its centre, where huge cliffs, principally of the Old Red sandstone formation, rise precipitously from the margin on either side. On the east side are those of Oulough. The broad surfaces of the rocks are beautifully pictured with a map-like coating of *Lecidæ* and *Lecanoræ*, and on those rocks, within a limited circuit, and at a distance of about 50 yards from the water, the *Geomalaci*, on a misty or showery day, may be noticed quiescently stretched, their richly maculated character being strikingly conspicuous. On the opposite side is the romantic little glen of Limnavar, and on similar rocks, at the same range from the water, *Geomalacus* is again met with, particularly the white variety, but more sparingly than at Oulough. On no other rocks around the lake or the country are they to be observed."

It is peculiar to the locality given. An allied species occurs in Portugal.

Genus Testacella.

The above generic appellation is derived from the diminutive of *Testa*, a shell or covering. The distinctive characters of the genus have already been given at p. 69.

Testacella haliotidea—(*the Ear-shaped Testa-*

cella) (Pl. VI., fig. 38).—This slug is of a dirty yellow colour, sometimes uniformly black, rarely pale yellow; spotted with brownish specks, mixed with pale orange along the margin of the foot; and is furnished with a small roundish oval shell, with a minute spire at the end of the tail (see fig. 14), which covers the mantle. A lateral furrow commences from near the tip of the shell by a double wavy line on both sides of the body, dividing the lateral portions of the animal in two unequal parts, until it terminates near the head. The surface of the body is granulated. This slug exhibits, as it were, a third pair of tentacles, by the protrusion of the corners of the lip; they resemble, but are scarcely so long as, the pair of tentacles above them. See fig. 14, show-

Fig. 14.—*Testacella haliotidea.*

ing a front view of the head; the centre figure represents the back view of a half-grown individual; the other, a side view of the shell on the tail; the respiratory orifice is also seen.

When crawling, the *Testacella* is about three inches in length.

The shell is oval, ear-shaped, depressed, rugous; striated in the lines of growth. Epidermis thin, readily peeling off; spire very short, of one whorl and a half; suture rather deep; summit shining, nearly in the middle, not detached from the columella. Aperture very large, rounded and dilated in front; interior nacreous, whitish, sometimes bluish. Shell one-quarter to two-fifths of an inch in length.

This species is very variable in its form, as regards the shell; sometimes nearly round, quadrangular, oval, &c. The variety *scutulum* differs essentially, in the shell being very acuminated posteriorly. This form was established in 1823, on specimens obtained at Lambeth, Surrey.

This species is found in kitchen and market gardens around London, Norwich, Gloucester, Taunton, Bristol, and in several localities in Devonshire, Tenby, and in the Channel Islands. In Ireland it has been taken at Youghal and Bandon. It also inhabits West Europe, Madeira, and the Canaries.

It is a highly curious animal, exclusively carnivorous, and is the dread of the earth-worm, which it follows in its burrow. Its organization is admirably adapted for its worm-hunting habits, its slender attenuated body enabling it to progress through the loose and broken soil. The worms are caught alive, and are swallowed whole, being drawn into the mouth by the introversive action of the tongue.

Dr. Ball observes, "I first became aware of this *Testacella* preying on worms by putting some of them in spirits, when they disgorged more of these animals than I thought they could possibly have contained : each worm was cut, but not divided, at regular intervals. I afterwards caught them in the act of swallowing worms four and five times their own length."

Testacella, and the other predaceous pulmoniferæ (*Daudebardia, Glandina,* and *Cylindrella*), do not possess horny jaws. The lingual ribbon is very large and wide, composed of about fifty transverse rows, which are oblique, and descend towards the middle; the teeth are conical, regu-

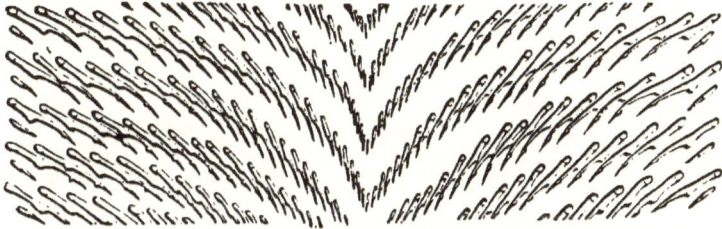

Fig. 15.—Part of the lingual ribbon of *T. haliotidea.*

larly curved, barbed at the point, and having a projection on the middle of the posterior side, from which the remainder thickens; the teeth diminish in size towards the centre; there are 51 in each row.

The animal, while engaged in laying its eggs, about ten in number, draws the head and tentacles in; the reproductive orifice is situated on

the right side behind and near the upper tentacle.   The eggs are oval, inflated at the middle,
hard, and opaque, with a calcareous shell, and
resemble the eggs of some reptiles ; when placed
before a fire, or even exposed in a dry atmosphere, they in a few minutes explode with a
loud crack.   The mollusk lays its eggs, ten to
fifteen in number, in a subterranean gallery
during the months of May, June, and July ; the
eggs are isolated 'one from the other, and are
not united in a mass, as in the true slugs ; the
young *Testacelles* are excluded in from twenty-
five to thirty days.   The food of the young slugs
consists of small worms, and the white, slender,
vermiform animals which live upon putrefying
vegetables.   They do not grow so rapidly as the
Limaces.

The *Testacellæ*, though subterranean in
their habits, may be met with at the surface
during the autumnal months, and before day-
break in April ; in winter, they bury from one
to two feet deep in the soil, and " form a kind
of cocoon in the ground by the exudation of

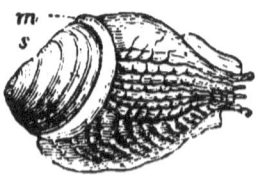

Fig. 16 —*T. Maugei*, just
disturbed from its sleep.

mucus.   If this cell is
broken, the animal may be
seen completely shrouded in
its thin, opaque, white mantle
(fig. 16, *m*), which rapidly
contracts until it extends but

Plate VI.

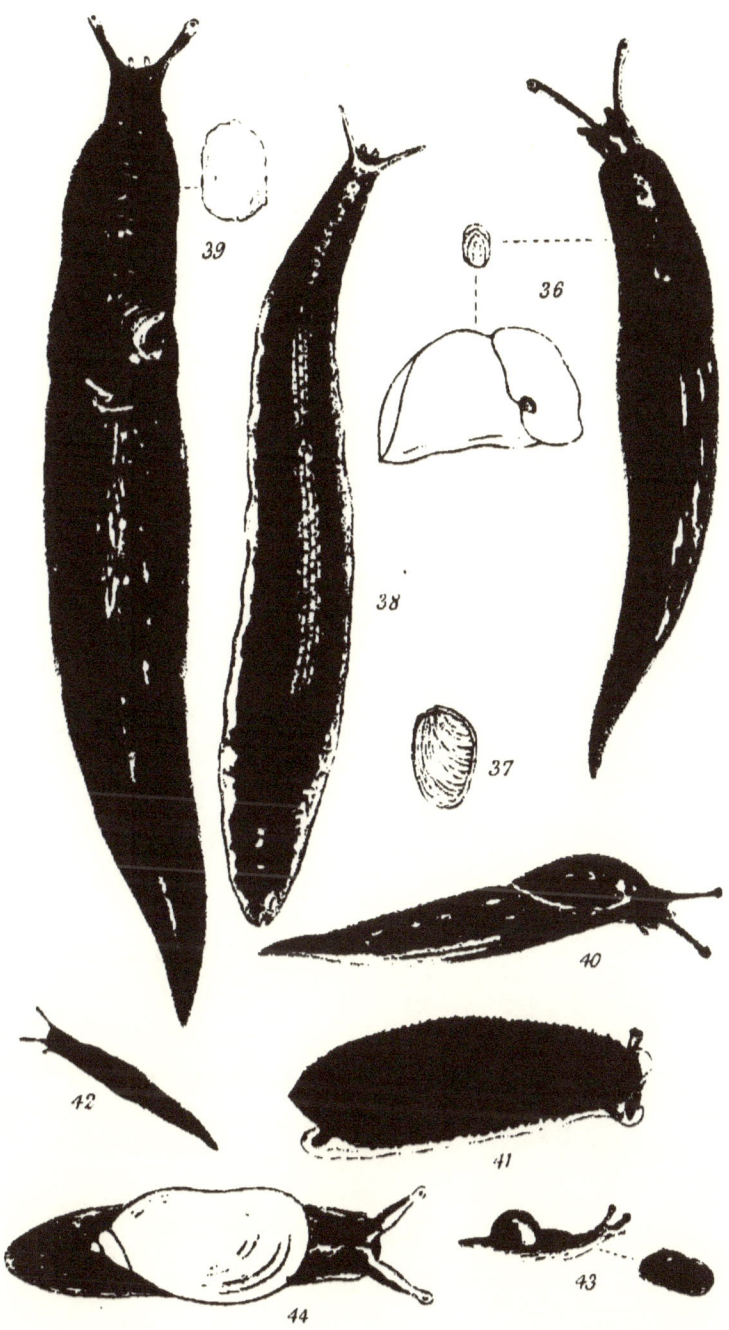

a little way beyond the margin of the shell (s)."
—*Woodward.*

Testacella appears to live five or six years.

TESTACELLA MAUGEI (Pl. VI., fig. 37), a kindred
species, is a native of the South-west of Europe,
and is confined to the coast; it was imported to
Bristol about the year 1830, where it is now
very plentiful, and has since been found at
Devizes. The slug is of a dark brown colour;
its shell, which is represented in Pl. VI., fig. 37,
is larger and more cylindrical than that of *T.
haliotidea.*

FAMILY ONCIDIADÆ.

The above group is allied to the true slugs,
and was founded to receive certain slug-like
animals destitute of any shell, and completely
covered by a leathery mantle. The species are
almost all inhabitants of tropical countries, many
of them living on the sea-shores, others in
marshes and woods. The family is represented
by one British species—

ONCIDIUM CELTICUM (Pl. VI., fig. 41).—The
body is oblong, covered with short, thick, convex
tubercles; it possesses only one pair of retractile
horns, which bear the eyes. The dental formula
is $\frac{51 \cdot 1 \cdot 51}{70}$.

This species frequents the sea-shore, and

though living in immediate contact with marine conditions, is truly pulmoniferous ; it occurs on the rocks at West Comb, in Lantivet Bay, between Polperro and Fowey, Cornwall, where it was discovered by Mr. Couch. They congregate in little groups about a foot or so from the margin of the sea where the waves break over them, ascending and descending so as to maintain their distance as the tides fluctuate.

A few words more as to the methods by which slugs may be preserved :—As regards the internal shell, it may be obtained by making a crucial incision in the shield, taking care not to cut down upon the calcareous plate, which can then be removed without difficulty. The animals can only be conserved by keeping them in some preservative fluid ; but the great object to keep in view, is to have the slug naturally extended. Most fluids contract the slugs when they are immersed in them. The slugs should be killed whilst crawling, by plunging them into a solution of corrosive sublimate, or into benzine. Models in wax or dough are sometimes substituted for the animals. A writer in the *Naturalist* gives a process for the preservation of slugs, which he states to answer admirably, and to be very superior to spirit, glycerine, creosote, and other solutions :—
" Make a cold saturated solution of *corrosive sublimate ;* put it into a deep wide-mouthed bottle ;

then take the slug you wish to preserve, and let it
crawl on a long slip of card. When the tentacles
are fully extended, plunge it suddenly into the solution; in a few minutes it will die, with the tentacles fully extended in the most life-like manner;
so much so, indeed, that if taken out of the fluid
it would be difficult to say whether it be alive or
dead. The slugs thus prepared should not be
mounted in spirit, as it is apt to contract and dis-
colour them. A mixture of one and a half parts of
water and one part of glycerine I find to be the
best mounting fluid. It preserves the colour
beautifully, and its antiseptic qualities are unex-
ceptional. A good-sized test-tube answers better
than a bottle for putting them up, as it admits
of closer examination of the animal. The only
drawback to this process is, that unless the solution is of sufficient strength, and unless the tentacles are extruded when the animal is immersed,
it generally, but not invariably, fails. Some slugs
appear to be more susceptible to the action of
the fluid than others; and it generally answers
better with full-grown than with young specimens.
But if successful, the specimens are as satisfac-
tory as could be desired; and, even if unsuccessful,
they are a great deal better than those preserved
in spirit; for, although the tentacles may not be
completely extruded, they are more or less so."

FAMILY HELICIDÆ (*Land Snails*).

The appellation of this wide-spread family of the Land Snails is derived from *Helix*, a snail, the typical genus of the group. The *Helicidæ* · are provided with an external spirally-coiled shell, capable of containing the entire animal. The body is conformable with the shell, and is distinct from the foot. The head of the snail is short and retractile, furnished with two pairs of cylindrical tentacles; the tentacles of the upper pair are the longest, and bear the eyes at their summits.

The snail and slug have both the power of drawing in their horns on being touched. We shall now proceed to explain " *how this is done ;*" for the snail can be examined more conveniently. On lifting our snail, the head and tentacles are retracted; but not doubting the efficacy of the words of the old doggerel, we admonish the snail "to come out of his hole." And we observe that the tentacle is lengthened by gradually unfolding itself, and not by being pushed out from the base. Each tentacle is a hollow cylinder (see fig. 17), to the apex of which is attached a muscle (*g*), arising from the retractor muscle (*m*) of the foot, and by its contraction the tentacle is simply inverted and retracted, like the finger of a tight glove; its protrusion, on the other hand, is effected by the alternate

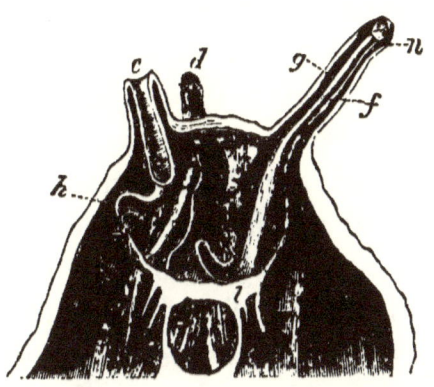

Fig. 7.—Structure of the tentacles in *Helix*.
a, *b*, *c*, *d*, Tentacles in different states of protrusion; *l*, brain mass;
f, *h*, nerves of tentacles; *g*, muscle of tentacle; *n*, eye. (*Owen.*)

contraction of the circular bands of muscle which compose the walls of the tentacle.

The *mouth* of the snail is armed with a horny semicircular jaw, which, by pressing against the floor of the mouth, cuts off the fragments of its vegetable food. The jaw presents various forms in the several species. The lingual ribbon comprises a central inconspicuous row, and two lateral rows with numerous teeth. The teeth differ from those of the slugs (*Limacidæ*), in that the apices of the lateral teeth, as they approach the margin, bifurcate and become serrated. However, those of *Vitrina* and *Helicella* resemble those of *Arion* and *Limax*.

Snails are vegetable-feeders, but some exhibit carnivorous propensities, the objects preyed upon being worms and small beetles; yet, on the other hand, the larvæ and imago of many beetles are the aggressors and not the victims. Snails also furnish food to the thrush, blackbird, starling, &c., the smaller species being swallowed entire; of the larger kinds the shell is broken on a stone, and the snail extracted. The domestic fowl will also feed upon them.

The *respiratory orifice* is seen on the right side, beneath the margin of the shell, when the snail is in motion. The *reproductive orifice*, as in the slugs, is situated near the base of the right upper tentacle. The eggs of most of the *Helicidæ* are globular in shape, and transparent or opaque; some are enveloped in a hard calcareous shell. They are usually laid in the summer, and vary in number from ten to one hundred, according to the species, either isolated or united together into a mass. The young appear at the end of about fifteen to twenty days, and attain about a third of their full size before hybernating, and usually complete their shell on their attaining their first year. The Helices do not live to a venerable age, for the majority of the species apparently do not survive the second winter.

Mr. E. J. Lowe communicated to the Royal Society, in 1854, observations he made on the growth of shells of land snails. The facts arrived

at were, that the shells of the *Helicidæ* increase
but little for a considerable period, never arriving
at maturity before the animal has *once* become
dormant. The shells do not grow whilst the
animal itself remains dormant, and the growth
is very rapid when it does take place. Most
species bury themselves in the ground to increase the dimensions of the shells. In illus-
tration follows here one of his experiments :—
"A pair of *Helix aspersa* had deposited their eggs,
which began to hatch on the 20th of June;
these young ones grew but little during the
summer. They buried themselves in the soil
on the 10th of October, coming again to the
surface on the 5th of April, *not having grown
during the winter*. In May they buried themselves with their *heads downwards* (in winter
they and other species buried themselves with
the *head upwards*), appearing again in a week
double the size. This process was carried on at
about fortnightly intervals until the 18th of July,
when they were almost fully grown.

"The process of growth *within the ground*
takes place with *Helix nemoralis*, *H. virgata*, and
H. hispida. But *H. rotundata* burrows into decayed
wood to increase the size of its shell; whilst
Helicella radiatula appears to remain on decaying
blades of grass; and *Pupa umbilicata*, *Clausilia
rugosa*, and *Bulimus obscurus* bury their *heads*

only to increase their shells. With respect to *Helicella cellaria, H. lucida,* and *H. nitidula,* it was not satisfactorily ascertained whether their heads were buried during the process of growth."

The *habits* of the British *Helices* vary with the species; they are all terrestrial; the majority of them are denizens of woods and shady places, climbing trees or rocks, or concealed among moss and under stones; others affect open heaths and pastures; a few are, as it were, domesticated; and *Helix aspersa* has the greatest claim for the title of the " Domesticated Snail ;" some others live on plants growing on the margins of pools, &c.

Independently of changes of temperature, the land snails have the power of becoming dormant at will. If a snail be deprived of food by placing it in a box, it will attach itself by a thin parchment-like secretion, or *epiphragm,* and will remain, if undisturbed, in a torpid state for a lengthened period. There is an account of a snail that thus lived without food for fifteen years. The snail in such cases may be resuscitated by plunging it into lukewarm water. In their native haunts, they are found in this state of inactivity during the summer season, when there is continued drought, but on the first shower they recover and move about in search of food. Such as live in exposed situations necessarily become inactive during the heat of the day, but are up and doing soon after the dew begins to fall. For these reasons a collector should remember, "it is the early bird that catches the worm," and be on the alert after rain.

Cold acts much in the same respect as heat, for in all temperate latitudes the majority of the *Helicidæ* hybernate; they then form a more dense epiphragm, and retreat farther into the interior of the shell than during their daily repose; in a few species the epiphragm is strengthened with carbonate of lime. During this winter sleep the animal functions are nearly suspended; respiration is still carried on, and air is admitted to the animal by a minute perforation in the epiphragm opposite the respiratory orifice.

Land shells are most abundant on limestone soils, which are most congenial to their existence and perpetuation; and in explanation I would observe: firstly, that the shell is composed almost entirely of carbonate of lime; secondly, the plants upon which the snail feeds are the sources from whence the mineral matters are derived thirdly, that plants affecting calcareous soils contain proportionately a larger amount of salts than those inhabiting clayey or sandy soils, and such are therefore in greater request among molluscan life; so also many species of horse-tails, and grasses which contain a large percentage of earthy salts, are much frequented by land snails.

Many mollusks are found in every situation and on every variety of soil, while others are to be found only in particular habitats.

The geological peculiarity of a district influences the distribution of land shells much more than geographical distribution. Thus, the majority of the snails occur throughout the length and breadth of Great Britain; of the remainder, those that are peculiar to the South of England flourish on soils derived from chalk and oolitic limestones. And the fact that a large portion of the life of the mollusk is passed in a state of hybernation, when the influence of climatical peculiarity is scarcely felt, accounts for the absence of any striking difference in the land molluscan fauna of the two opposite extremities of our island.

The British species are collected with advantage in the autumn, when they are full grown; the winter rains destroy much of the original beauty of the shells.

Land and fresh-water snails may be killed with boiling water, and the animals may be removed from their shells by the aid of a bent pin; *Clausiliæ*, *Helicellæ*, &c., which retire too far to be reached by this ordinary expedient, may be killed by placing them in tepid water, and adding gradually hot water; the animals may then be partially removed. The shells should be well dried, to remove the moisture and harden the soft parts remaining; but the heat must not be too great, or else the shells will be discoloured, and are liable to be broken. And, further, the specimens should be well dried before placing them in the cabinet, which should be in a well-ventilated place, free from damp; for their freshness and beauty are apt to be lost by the growth of fungi upon their surfaces.

The following synoptical table represents the genera into which the family *Helicidæ* is divided :—

1.	Shell oval ... ... *Succinea*
	„ globular or depressed, mouth transverse ... 2
	„ more or less cylindrical, mouth longitudinal 4
2.	Shell glassy, outer lip thin 3
	„ not glassy, outer lip usually reflected ... *Helix*
3.	Shell imperforated ... ... *Vitrina*
	„ umbilicated ... ... *Helicella*
4.	Shell fusiform, sinistral 5
	„ turreted 6
	„ subcylindrical... 7
	„ oblong 8
5.	Aperture with a clausium ... ... *Clausilia*
	No clausium, aperture toothless ... ... *Balea*
6.	Columella truncated in front ... ... *Achatina*
	Front entire ... ... *Bulimus acutus*
7.	Shell dextral, animal with four tentacles ... *Pupa*
	„ sinistral or dextral, lower tentacles obsolete ... ... *Vertigo*
8.	Shell polished 9
	„ dull... ... ... *Bulimus*
9.	Aperture toothless ... ... *Zua*
	„ denticulated ... ... *Azeca*

H 2

Genus Vitrina.

The distinctive generic title is derived from the Latin word *vitrum,* glass. This generic group is a connecting link between the Slugs and the true Snails or *Helices ;* for it has the lingual dentition and the shield-like mantle of *Limax* and the globular external shell of *Helix.* They appear to be occasionally animal-feeders, like the slugs, a propensity equally possessed by some of the *Helices. Vitrina* may be readily distinguished from *Helicella,* by the absence of an umbilicus ; for all the shells of species of the latter are per-forated. The genus is represented in Britain by only one species :—

VITRINA PELLUCIDA—(*the Green Glassy Snail*) (Pl. VI., fig. 43).—The body of this snail is elon-gated, too large to allow of the animal retracting completely into the shell. The mantle is pro-duced into a shield and reflected over the front of the shell when the animal crawls, and furnished with a tongue-like lobe on the right side; the lingual teeth are like those of *Limax,* of 100 rows of 75 each, and the jaw resembles that of the true slugs and cellar snails, in being strongly arched from before backwards, produced into a beak, smooth or nearly so.

The beautiful greenish-glassy shell of this

species is very thin, depressed and compressed, composed of three whorls : the last one is large. The aperture is oval, with a thin edge. There is no umbilicus. The breadth is about one-fourth of an inch, and the height one-twelfth and a half. It varies in colour and shape. The green transparency gives place to a white opacity in dead shells that have been long exposed.

The little *Vitrinæ* are thorough gourmands; their appetite never fails them. These little snails feed on mosses and fallen leaves; vegetable substances in a state of decomposition are preferred by them. But it must not be supposed that they are exclusively vegetarians; on the contrary, they are often carnivorous, and not only satisfy their hunger with dead prey, but even with living prey. The observations made upon this little species by M. le Dr. Baudon are very curious and interesting. He writes, in his " Catalogue des Moll. de l'Oise," 1862 : "I placed a great number of individuals under a bell-glass with other mollusks, taking care to provide them with rocks, leaves, and mosses, upon which they lived. One of the Vitrines attacked and devoured a *Helicella cellaria* ; two *Zonites candidissimus*, killed by their bites, were devoured in two days. . . . . . I then placed under the glass a piece of raw mutton, of the size of a hazel-nut; five minutes had not elapsed, when the Vitrines in the immediate vicinity quitted the leaves, which they were then eating ; . . . . from all quarters were the Vitrines seen marching on, leaving the holes where they had been reposing . . . . . it was a general *rendezvous*.　One that was feeding upon the remains of *Helicella cellaria* abandoned its victim to satisfy the craving of a newly acquired taste.　I remarked, at this moment, a veritable expression in their tentacles ; when the nervous ganglion had received the odoriferous impression, the horns were no longer swayed to and fro, but steadily fixed on the object which attracted them.　It is believed that life is concentrated in these delicate stalks.　Animation has been pointed out in the ear of certain beings of a superior organization ; why may it not be found to exist, though in a less degree, in the tentacle of a snail,—principal seat of its physiognomy ! After its heavy meal, the Vitrine takes no food for many days, and its activity is not so great as when its aliment is vegetable."

Vitrina pellucida is abundant in suitable localities,—humidity is essential to it,—among moss and decaying leaves in woods and glens ; under stones and herbage in meadows on the coast-line, and to a great altitude in the mountain glens. Shelter, it apparently needs none, further than what is imperfectly provided for it by its own comparatively small shell ; for it may be seen actively in motion at all times of the year, and not more frequently at other seasons than during the winter months. I, as well as many others, have seen this hardy creature creeping upon the snow.

Bouchard-Chautereaux, a French conchologist, who made the habits of the land and fresh-water snails of his country objects of especial study, says that the eggs are not laid until towards the close of the year, and that the young attain their adult condition at the end of the eighth or tenth month; and he is of opinion that they do not live longer than from twelve to fifteen months.

GENUS HELICELLA (*diminutive of Helix, a Snail*).

The shells of this genus are thin, shining, and depressed (except in *H. fulva*); the peristome is sharp and not reflected, and the aperture obliquely crescent-shaped.

The animal of *Helicella* has an elongated extremely compressed foot, which extends far behind; the upper tentacles are long, the lower ones short, all terminating in a knob. The lingual dentition is somewhat intermediate between *Vitrina* and *Helix*, and resembles *Limax* in the long projecting single apex to the edge teeth; the teeth, however, are not so numerous (see fig. 19). The jaw is, like that of *Limax, Vitrina,*

and *Succinea,* smooth, with a more or less prominent beak in the middle
of its lower edge (see fig.
18, which represents the
horny jaw or buccal plate
of the cellar snail).

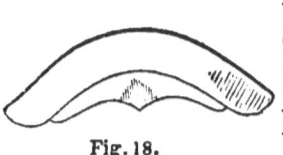

Fig. 18.

When the animal crawls, the shell is balanced
nearly horizontally on its back. The tentacles
are protruded and withdrawn with surprising
quickness. The species feed on vegetable substances, and inhabit damp or shady places, as
under stones, or among grass or moss.

The species are very difficult to distinguish;
I have given therefore full descriptions of each.
The following analytical table may be found
useful :—

1. { Shell depressed, umbilicus apparent   2
   { „   trochiform, umbilicus minute   ... ... *H. fulva*

2. { Opacity around the umbilicus...   3
   { No opacity   4

3. { Umbilicus large ; very clouded below...   *H. cellaria*
   { Upper surface more convex, dull ... ...   *H. nitidula*
   { Shell smaller, surface shining... ... ...   *H. alliaria*

4. { Shell white   5
   { „   horn-coloured   6

5. { Whorls not rapidly enlarging... ... ... *H. crystallina*
   { Last whorl capacious   ... ... *H. pura*

6. { Umbilicus very large   ... ...   *H. excavata*
   { Umbilicus moderate   7

7. { Surface radiately striated   ... ... *H. radiatula*
   { „   transversely wrinkled... ... ...   *H. nitida*

HELICELLA CELLARIA—(*the Cellar Snail*) (Pl. VII., fig. 63)—is one of our common shells, universally distributed throughout Great Britain; beneath stones, about walls, in gardens, and woods. It has a predilection for wet situations, and is not unfrequently found in damp cellars. It has been introduced into Portland, Maine, U.S., where it is rare, in cellars and gardens.

The shell is flattened, with the spire very little raised; the colour is a dirty yellow or pale horn, upper surface rather opaque, under surface clouded with opaque white, especially about the umbilicus, which is very large, and exposes the second whorl; the whorls are five or five and a half in number; the aperture is obliquely crescent-shaped, rather broader than high. It is the largest of the British species, having an average diameter of two-fifths to half an inch, but attaining even to three-fourths of an inch.

The dental formula is $\frac{17 \cdot 1 \cdot 17}{38}$. "The central plate is very long and narrow, with three teeth, occupying nearly the centre of the plate; the

Fig. 19.

first four *laterals* are irregular in shape, apparently bidentated; the *uncini* are long, single, and aculeate " (see fig. 19).—*Morse.* The horny jaw of the cellar snail is represented in fig. 18, p. 104.

Species of the genus *Helicella* are preyed upon by thrushes, blackbirds, and starlings, which may be found perfect in the stomachs of these birds.

HELICELLA ALLIARIA—(*the Garlic Snail*) (Pl. VII., fig. 59)—is a widely-diffused species, but not so abundant as the last, and readily distinguished from it and the other species of the genus by the diffusion of a garlic odour, which may frequently guide the collector to its retreat. The emission of the peculiar odour is not always obvious, but may generally be excited by pressing the animal with a stalk of grass; or on immersion in hot water, those that may have retained it, do not generally fail to emit in death the yellowish fluid, which appears to be the source of this alliaceous smell.

It frequents the same habitats as the last, and attains a great elevation on mountains.

Shell flattened, with the spire very little raised; colour pale amber or horn, transparent, very shining; around the umbilicus there is a little opacity; upper surface smooth, or but slightly wrinkled; whorls three and a half to four; umbilicus moderately large, scarcely exposing the second whorl; aperture crescent-shaped, not very oblique, rather broader than high; diameter one-fifth to a quarter of an inch. The dental formula is $\frac{12\cdot1\cdot12}{3\,5}$.

HELICELLA NITIDULA — (*the Dull Snail*) (Pl. VII., fig. 60)—is generally distributed, but not a very common shell. Under stones, about old walls, among mosses in glens and sheltered places.

The shell is flattened, with the spire somewhat raised (more so than either of the preceding); colour that of horn, not shining, and darker than that of *H. cellaria* or *H. alliaria*, dull, semi-transparent above, more transparent below, except about the umbilicus, where there is a slight white opacity; upper surface irregularly wrinkled or striated; the striæ interrupted by the sutures, and not continued from whorl to whorl, as in *H. radiatula*; whorls four and a half, with a well-defined suture; umbilicus large, exposing the previous whorl; aperture crescent-shaped, a little oblique, rather broader than high; diameter three-eighths to three-tenths of an inch. The dental formula is $\frac{32\cdot1\cdot32}{5\,5}$.

HELICELLA PURA—(*the Delicate Snail*) (Pl. VII., fig. 55)—is not uncommon among moss, decaying leaves, stumps of trees, and under stones in woods and pastures.

The shell is flattened, with the spire very slightly raised; colour white, rarely very pale amber; transparent, not very shining; under surface without opacity; upper surface smooth or slightly wrinkled; whorls three and a half to four, rather flattened above; body whorl much larger than that preceding it; sutures well defined, deep and narrow; umbilicus moderately large; aperture oblique, crescent-shaped, broader than high; diameter one-tenth to one-sixth of an inch.

HELICELLA CRYSTALLINA—(*the Crystalline Snail*) (Pl. VII., fig. 58)—is common among moss, herbage, decaying leaves, and under stones in woods, pastures, and hedgerows.

The shell is flattened, with the spire very slightly raised; colour white, or with a slight greenish tinge, very shining and transparent; under surface without opacity; upper surface smooth or slightly wrinkled; whorls four and a half to five, of gradual increase, the body whorl being but little larger than that preceding it; whorls flattened above; sutures well defined; umbilicus very small; aperture not very oblique, crescent-shaped, about as broad as high; diameter from one-twelfth to one-eighth of an inch.

HELICELLA EXCAVATA—(*the Excavated Snail*) (Pl. VII., fig. 52).—The shell is depressed, subglobular; colour that of darkish horn, shining and transparent; under surface not obscured by any white opacity; upper surface strongly and regularly striated, the striæ being continued over the base, but not so well defined on this aspect; whorls five to five and a half, well rounded, especially on the inferior surface; umbilicus very large and capacious, disclosing all the whorls; aperture rather small, lunate, as broad as high; diameter three-fourths of an inch.

This species inhabits woods, about the decaying stumps of trees, and among dead leaves and moss. It is peculiar to Great Britain, and is recorded from Yorkshire, Northumberland (Alnwick), Durham, and other counties in the north of England; South of Scotland; Tunbridge; Wootton, near Gloucester; Sandown, Isle of Wight; and Clifden, co. Galway.

HELICELLA RADIATULA—(*the Rayed Snail*) (Pl. VII., fig. 61).—This is a minute and well-marked species.

Its favourite habitat is among grass and moss in damp pastures, under stones, and among moss, grass, and decaying trunks of trees in woods.

The shell is flattened, spire scarcely raised; colour deep horn or amber, shining, transparent; under surface without any white opacity; upper surface regularly and distinctly striated, the striæ continued from whorl to whorl, and not interrupted by the suture; whorls three and a half to four; body whorl much larger than that preceding it; umbilicus moderately large; aperture oblique, crescent-shaped, broader than high; diameter from one-twelfth to one-sixth of an inch.

HELICELLA NITIDA—(*the Glossy Snail*) (Pl. VII., fig. 54).—The shell is flattened, with the spire somewhat raised, more so than in *H. nitidula*, of a greyish-brown colour, glossy and semi-transparent, rather strongly transversely wrinkled; there is no whiteness or opacity beneath; whorls five; the umbilicus large and deep; aperture oblique, roundish, longer than broad; diameter three-twelfths of an inch; height nearly half the breadth.

The animal is bluish-black, and the shell when it contains the body appears of a dark chocolate-brown. This species differs from *H. nitidula* in its greater convexity, stronger striations, wider umbilicus, and in being destitute of an opacity underneath.

It is not a common species, inhabiting moist places among herbage, on the margins of muddy streams, ditches, and marshy places.

HELICELLA FULVA—(*the Fulvous Snail*) (Pl. VII., fig. 56).—This species is easily recognized by its conical shell with a shallow ill-defined umbilicus. The shell is thin, glossy, semi-transparent, and horn-coloured, as in the other *Helicellæ.*

The diameter of the pyramidal shell is a tenth of an inch, and the height nearly the same. The dental formula is $\frac{2\,2 \cdot 1 \cdot 2\,2}{7\,0}$.

It is widely distributed, though seldom met with in abundance in any one locality. It inhabits beneath stones in quarries and old walls, and among moss and herbage in woods and moist pastures.

There is a very striking resemblance between *H. fulva* and *H. chersina* of America, yet these species have never been united.

All the above-mentioned species of *Helicella* are fossilized in the Pleistocene fresh-water marls at Copford, Clacton, &c.

Genus Helix.

The British *Helices* are comprised in 25 species, which I have arranged into artificial groups, founded upon characters afforded by the adult shells. These are exhibited in the following table, which is merely intended to assist the student in discovering the species :—

1. { Shell imperforated,—*H. aspersa, H. nemoralis* and *H. hortensis*
   { „ umbilicated   2

2. { Shell more or less globular   3
   { „ depressed   7

3. { Mouth with an internal band   4
   { No internal band ; minutely umbilicated   5

4. {
   Shell with coloured bands,—*H. Pisana, H. virgata,* and
       H. caperata
     „ uniformly coloured, more or less hairy, at least in
       the young, —*H. Cartusiana, H. Cantiana, H.
       rufescens, H. concinna, H. hispida,* and *H.
       sericea*

5. {
   Shell subglobose, thin, and very transparent,—*H. revelata*
       and *H. fusca*
     „ globosely conical   6

6. {
   Shell with raised epidermis,—*H. aculeata* and *H. lamel-*
       lata
     „ very large, banded,—*H. arbustorum* and *H. pomatia*

7. {
   Peristome united all round,—*H. pulchella* and *H. lapicida*
     „   incomplete   8

8. {
   Aperture toothed ... ...   *H. obvoluta*
     „ with no denticulations, outer lip not reflected, 9

9. {
   Shell banded, large ... ...   *H. ericetorum*
     „ not banded,—*H. rotundata, H. rupestris,* and *H.*
       pygmæa

HELIX ASPERSA—(*Common Snail*) (Pl. VII., fig. 57).—The shell of this species is globular, with a wrinkled surface; the colour is yellowish-brown, with five spiral dark bands, traversed by white zigzag streaks; the whorls are four in number, and the aperture is obliquely oval, with a white reflected lip. It exhibits great variation in colour and marking, but its wrinkled epidermis is a sufficiently distinctive feature.

Reversed monstrosities occur, as also others with an elongated spire, with the whorls produced and separated from one another, so that the shell resembles a ram's horn.

Dr. S. P. Woodward has in his possession " an adult shell with a second half-grown individual fixed to its spire, and partly imbedded in the suture of the body whorl. The epiphragm remains in the exposed part of the small shell's aperture, showing that it had died during the first hybernation, whilst its neighbour had survived, and not getting free from the incubus of the empty house of the deceased, had partially enveloped it in the course of its growth to maturity." M. d'Orbigny bred for many years in succession from a reversed monstrosity of *H. aspersa*—one of our commonest and most generally-known snails.

Theoretically considered, there are no useless animals. All the beings disseminated over the surface of the earth must be regarded as playing each their part in the economy of nature, from the single fact of their existence. They, by their incessant co-operation, maintain that admirable, unalterable equilibrium of the natural world. But practically considered it is another thing; and in inhabited districts a distinction arises as to what are the useful and what the injurious animals Man finds around him. Against the latter, wrongfully or justifiably, a war of extermination is declared, whilst the others are surrounded by all the protection they appear to require.

The agriculturist, and especially the horticul-

I

turist, count among the former group the slugs and snails : even our present acquaintance, *H. aspersa*, is regarded by them as a great pest in the gardens, devouring vegetables with the greatest avidity, and is treated accordingly. Many of these enemies have been mentioned ; some still remain to have their misdeeds published to the world. Those snails which derive their nourishment from culinary and cultivated plants belong to the second category. The means to be employed for their destruction are :—

1st.—By the aid of their natural enemies. Thus many insects, especially of the genera *Drylus, Lampyris, Staphylinus, Sylpha*, attack the terrestrial species, and deposit their eggs in the substance of the snail's body. Ducks, geese, fowls, thrushes, blackbirds, prey upon them ; the hedgehog devours with avidity *Helices* and *Bulimi*.

2nd.—By protecting the trees and plants from their attacks,—encircling them with absorbent powders,—washing the walls with a weak solution of corrosive sublimate.

3rd.—By the destruction of the eggs and individuals : and to do this, dig deep the soil, leaving it exposed to the sun, for some days, before consigning to it the grain and plants. The individuals may be decoyed, gathered, and destroyed by throwing into lime-water, &c.

Yet a few of these humble and persecuted objects may be ranked among the useful class of animals : some, as *H. pomatia, aspersa, nemoralis, hortensis, Pisana,* serving for food ; and recently they have silently rendered a great service to man, in giving to Dr. de Lemare his precious *Helicine.* This material is the concentrated mucilage of snails ; and by means of this preparation, known under the names of the syrup of snails, *pommade* of snails, and *helicine,* this learned physician is stated to have radically cured, in the last few years, numerous cases of phthisis. From French newspaper reports it would appear that the effects of the employment of *Helicine* are truly marvellous. One provincial paper writes, that the *Helicine* of Dr. de Lemare is for phthisis what *quinine* is for intermittent fevers.

In this country this species, boiled in milk, is still used by some in their domestic pharmacopœia, and great faith is placed in it as a cure for pulmonary complaints ; but, so far as the experience of medical men goes, it does not appear to be a remedy of any efficacy. Like many other articles of a peculiar and out-of-the-way character, a dose of snail-broth may be productive of good, provided the patient indulging in its use is firmly convinced of its salutary powers. Remedies of the above nature in use among the lower classes owe their popularity to a vulgar creed, that whatever is disgusting and nauseous, must necessarily be fraught with healing virtues. Dr. Gray writes, that " the glassmen of New-castle once a year have a snail-feast, and that they generally collect the snails themselves in the fields and hedges the Sunday before the feast." The working population of Lancashire have a reputation for the like custom.

In the South of France an annual snail-feast is held on Ash-Wednesday, on which day there is a very large consumption of the very unsub-stantial and indigestible flesh of snails. Vendors are seen standing in the streets with great ham-pers full of *Helix aspersa* and *H. nemoralis;* the former of the two is preferred. They are sold at the rate of 25 *centimes*, or 2½d., per 100. From seven to eight thousand of *H. aspersa* form part of the provisions of a ship leaving the port of Bordeaux for a long voyage. Nearly all the snails that constitute so important a part in the live stock of ships come from one commune, that of Cauderan, which is infested by them.

Mr. J. G. Jeffreys, quoting Lister, writes that " the fluid which exudes so copiously from the body of *H. aspersa* when pricked, was used in his time in bleaching wax for artistic purposes, as well as in making a firm cement, mixed with the white of an egg." In the London streets I have frequently seen a man vending an article, stated to be a compound of the juices of this snail and the green matter of ivy-leaves, as a plaster for corns.

Perforations of two or three inches in depth on the under surface of projecting masses of limestone, in which *H. aspersa*, *H. nemoralis*, and a few other species, are found tenanting as winter-quarters, are regarded as the result of the constant resort to the one spot for shelter by the snails, winter after winter in the course of ages. It is usually accepted that the erosion is due to the action of the foot, aided by an acid secretion. Another theory is, that the snail works with its shell, after the manner of an auger. A more probable solution is, that the snails abrade the walls of these limestone cells with their tongues, for the purpose of obtaining the carbonate of lime. *H. aspersa* possesses 105 teeth on each transverse row, of which there are 135.

We must not forget the poetic allusion by Gay to the pretty conceits of the English rustic beauty, of the power of the snail to reveal to her the name of her destined lover. May-day morning is the auspicious occasion on which the tender-hearted maidens can read their fortunes in the meanderings of the snail :—

> Last May-day fair I search'd to find a snail,
> That might my secret lover's name reveal.

Upon a gooseberry-bush a snail I found
(For always snails near sweetest fruit abound) :
I seized the vermin, home I quickly sped,
And on the hearth the milk-white embers spread.
Slow crawl'd the snail ; and, if I right can spell,
In the soft ashes mark'd a curious L.
Oh ! may this wondrous omen lucky prove !
For L is found in Lubberkin and Love.

This species appears to be very susceptible of cold, retiring early to their winter-quarters in the cracks and holes of old walls and trees, and in other equally sheltered situations, where they are to be seen clustered together by their epiphragms, as if the gregarious propensity were induced for the purpose of communicating warmth to one another.

Within that house secure he hides,
When danger imminent betides,
Of storm, or other harm besides
              Of weather.—*Cowper.*

Helix aspersa is very universally distributed ; yet I find it to be a comparatively rare snail in the North of Ireland, and it is there only met with in the valleys, and in sheltered spots in the immediate vicinity of the sea, and always at low elevations. Fleming states that it occurs in Aberdeenshire, " here and there in the maritime and lower inland tracts, especially in gardens, about old walls, and on hedge-banks, but chiefly along the coast."

In the northern parts of Great Britain it seems thus to be partial to the vicinity of the sea. At Whitehaven it is found in innumerable quantities attached to a wall fronting the beach, and exposed to the sea-breeze. So, also, the late Mr. J. Thompson observed numbers of them on rocks subjected to the spray of the waves, which had bleached the portion of the shell thus exposed as white as it usually becomes in the progress of decay, although the animal inhabitants were all in the highest vigour.

The amours of this snail, as in fact of the other *Helices*, are conducted after a curious fashion. During the spring and summer the snails are furnished with spicula — crystalline darts, which they eject at each other; the tender passion is further excited by long-continued caresses with their horns, and they have been observed engaged in this love-making for the space of ten hours. The love-missiles are contained in a special pouch, and are peculiar to the genus *Helix;* their shape, dimensions, and number, vary in the several species. In *H. aspersa* they are half an inch long, hollow, and square at the base. If there be but the one use for these weapons, it would seem that the snail occasionally misses his mark; for Mr. Hyndman, of

Belfast, once found a spiculum of *H. nemoralis* stuck through a dandelion leaf.

The garden snail is the most prolific of the *Helices*, depositing from 100 to 110 eggs. The spot selected for the purpose of depositing these is under a stone, or piece of decaying wood, lying in some damp and unfrequented part of the garden, or it may be buried in the moist soil. The young snails appear at the end of from fifteen to thirty days, and at the end of the autumn are about the size of a hazel-nut, and attain their adult condition in the latter part of the following year.

HELIX NEMORALIS — (*the Wood Snail*) (Pl. VII., fig. 45).—The shell of this snail is familiar to all, and is one of our prettiest. It is either of a yellow or chocolate-brown, encircled with from one to five brownish spiral bands; of a globular form with a roundish aperture; the reflected margin is brown; the diameter is not quite an inch, and the height is about three-quarters.

The jaw of this snail is strongly arched, and

Fig. 20.—Jaw of *H. nemoralis.*

marked with five longitudinal ribs, which indent the edges of the plate. The lingual ribbon contains 135 rows of 100 teeth each.

Its specific name implies that it is a woodland species ; it is frequent though in our hedges and about rocks or hills ; it is certainly more maritime, and lives at greater altitudes, than the next species, to which it is closely allied.

The shell exhibits great variation in size, in the intensity of the colour, and in the size, disposition, and number of the bands. A French conchologist, M. Moquin-Tandon, characterized 77 varieties of this species; another author, M. A. Gras, has enumerated no less than 198. In general the varieties with five and three bands are the most common ; next with two, with one, and four : the same with regard to *H. hortensis.*

HELIX HORTENSIS—(*the Garden Snail*) (Pl. VII., fig. 47)—is regarded by many authors as a permanent variety of the last species, but it differs in a few particulars from it. The shell is always smaller, usually of a lighter colour and thinner, with a white reflected margin around the aperture. It is a common species everywhere in our gardens and hedgerows. The two species are not usually found living together. In the neighbourhood of Hastings, and other similarly situated localities, I have found *H. nemoralis* along the coast-line, feeding on *Ononis arvensis,* &c., and becoming uncommon inland, where it is replaced by the present species.

H. hortensis is subject also to many variations in colour. M. Moquin-Tandon distinguished forty-

six, and M. Bouillet ninety. One pretty variety
I have met with is of a white colour, with colourless bands. A more permanent variety, and by
some raised to the rank of a species under the
technical appellation of *H. hybrida*, is of a more
uniformly yellowish-brown colour, with a beautiful rosy lip, whitish towards the edge : it is local,
but not rare.

H. hortensis is a favourite food with thrushes and
blackbirds. Every country schoolboy is familiar
with the snail-hunting propensities of these birds.
In a country walk one may frequently see a large
stone surrounded by fractured snail shells ; these
are the slaughtering-blocks whereon the poor
snail is sacrificed for the welfare of our songsters
and their young progenies. The shells are very
systematically broken. The bird strikes the shell
upon the stone in such a position as to expose the
principal mass of the snail at about the commence-
ment of the last whorl, and the part immediately
above of the preceding whorl. The shells of
other snails, as *H. arbustorum, H. nemoralis,* and
H. aspersa, occur among the debris in the
thrushes' haunts ; the former not so often, on
account of its less frequency ; and the latter also,
because of the greater thickness of their shells.

The garden snail is found apparently indigenous on islands off the coast of Maine, North
America ; it inhabits Greenland.

HELIX PISANA—(*the Banded Snail*) (Pl. VIII., fig. 66).—The specific name, "Pisana," was given to this species from its having been first found at Pisa.

This species is the most beautiful of our snails. The shell is solid, moderately glossy, about a fourth of an inch in diameter, and half an inch high, with five whorls of yellowish-white ornamented with numerous brown spiral bands, interrupted by short oblique streaks of the same colour, giving the upper surface a speckled appearance.

The aperture is rounded, rose-coloured in the interior, with an internal rib : the umbilicus is narrow, nearly closed by the reflected margin of the lip. The dental formula is $\frac{3\cdot5\cdot1\cdot3\cdot5}{120}$.

In Great Britain it is only found on the coast-line. On the sand-banks between Tenby and Kilter Point it is very numerous. Another locality is St. Ives, where in the hot weather the snails have been observed buried in the sand at the roots of *Carex arenaria* to the depth of some inches. It also occurs abundantly near Dublin, and in Jersey. On the Continent it is confined to the southern countries, but it is found at Constantinople, with such western species as *H. Cartusiana*, *H. virgata*, and *H. ericetorum*.

HELIX VIRGATA—(*the Zoned Snail*) (Pl. VIII., fig. 80).—This snail, with *H. caperata*, *H. ericetorum*, and *Bulimus acutus*, affects the dry stunted

vegetation on downs and heaths.   It is generally
found in greater abundance on the sea-coast, but
occurs in many inland districts.   It is a very
abundant and gregarious species, adhering in
clusters to the stems of various plants.   During
the hot weather they bury themselves about the
roots of plants; but after a shower of rain they
appear in such abundance that they are supposed
by country folks to come down from the clouds
with the rain.

Helix virgata has the propensity of feeding upon
Coccinella and other small insects, and is itself,
with its congeners, accidentally eaten by sheep
pasturing on the downs and commons, where it
occurs in such profusion.   "For it is indeed impossible that the sheep can browse on the short
grass without devouring a prodigious quantity of
them, especially in the night, or after rain, when
they ascend the stunted blades;" and in the South
of England it is a prevalent, and probably a
correct opinion, that these snails contribute much
to the fattening of sheep.   The superiority of the
Dartmoor and Southdown mutton is presumed
to be attributable to the flavour imparted to it by
these mollusks.   The *distoma*, or fluke of sheep,
possibly may be derived from the embryonic
form which lives parasitically in the snail.

Some authors have remarked, from their own
observations, in particular localities, that it is

never found in company with *H. ericetorum*. This observation is not of general application.

The shell of the "zoned snail" is conical; white, or cream-colour; with a single dark-brown band in the middle of the last whorl, and with many smaller ones beneath. It varies much in colour and external markings. A pretty variety has two narrow brown bands on the under surface, between which is a row of brown spots, each connected by a narrow brown band. Within the aperture of the shell, and at a distance of two lines from its reflected margin, is a narrow but well-marked ridge, usually corresponding to that of the mouth, which is a purplish-brown.

The whorls are six in number, and the shell has an average diameter of a fourth of an inch. A few specimens collected by me in corn-fields on the chalk downs, near Eastbourne, have a breadth of seven-tenths of an inch. Mr. J. G. Jeffreys has seen specimens from Weymouth a tenth of an inch broader.

HELIX CAPERATA—(*the Wrinkled Snail*) (Pl. VIII., fig. 78).—So called from the numerous concentric rib-like striæ upon the whorls; it is further to be distinguished from *H. virgata* by its depressed spire and larger umbilicus, and is usually of a much smaller size. The colour of the shell is usually of a dull yellowish-white, with narrow brown bands. The spire is tipped

with black or brown, from which latter character
it is known by another name, that of *II. fasciolata*.
The dental formula is $\frac{2 5 \cdot 1 \cdot 2 5}{8 0}$. It is extremely
variable in colour, from white to reddish-brown,
and in the number and colour of the bands.

It is generally associated with the last species,
but is not so abundant; it is, however, more
widely distributed.

HELIX CANTIANA— (*the Kentish Snail*) (Pl.
VIII., fig. 64).—The shell of this snail is subglobose, thin, semi-transparent, and yellowish-
white, with a tinge of pale rose-colour, especially towards the aperture. The margin of the
aperture is thin and but slightly reflected, and
at a little distance from its edge is an internal
thick and white rib; there is a small narrow
and deep umbilicus; the whorls are six or seven
in number; the diameter of the shell is three-
fourths of an inch. Young shells want the
internal rib, and are clothed with short hairs,
which disappear in the adult. The dental formula is $\frac{4 0 \cdot 1 \cdot 4 0}{1 2 5}$.

H. Cantiana is a southern species in Europe,
and attains its northern limit in England; it is
indigenous in the south-eastern counties. It is
abundant on nettles, and plants in wet places,
and by ditches in Kent and Sussex, and in the
counties bordering the river Thames.

It is plentiful on the downs at Bedminster, &c.,

in the vicinity of Bristol; Swansea; and on the banks of the river Tyne, about Newcastle: in these localities it is said to have been introduced with ballast.

In the Bristol district it was first observed between Brislington and Keynsham, in 1825. Gardner, in his "Natural History of Stafford-shire," says, "it is not rare in the Dovesdale and Wetton valleys." And as it occurs also in North Gloucestershire, at Evesham, there is no reason to doubt that the Kentish snail is truly indigenous to the western counties of England.

HELIX CARTUSIANA — (Pl. VIII., fig. 70).—So called from its having been first discovered near a Carthusian Monastery; it is closely related to the Kentish snail, and possesses a white internal rib and an umbilicus, as in that species, but differs from it in its much smaller size, being about half an inch in diameter, more solid and not so glossy, nearly opaque; it is more depressed, and the umbilicus is minute.

It is found on the short herbage clothing the chalk downs of the Kentish and Sussex coasts. It appears to be confined to the neighbourhood of the sea, and to the chalk soil; though there are many favourable localities for it along the coast intervening between Folkestone and East-bourne, yet I have failed to find, though often sought for it. The same is true of *H. ericetorum* and *Cyclostoma elegans*. Now the strata embraced within that line of coast are composed of sandstones, sands, and clays belonging to the Greensand and Wealden formations, and the recent alluvial deposits.

Though much has been written for and against the restriction of snails to certain soils, nevertheless I adduce the above case as a very striking example in favour of the association of certain land shells to particular kinds of rocks, though not necessarily to any given formation.

The specific name is usually written *Carthusiana*, but Mr. J. G. Jeffreys thinks "the original spelling of *Cartusiana* ought to be retained."

HELIX RUFESCENS—(*the Rufous Snail*) (Pl. VIII., fig. 76).—So called from the rufous-brown of the shell. Though usually of this colour, yet it presents intermediate shades, even to a pure white.

The shell is depressed, slightly angular below, composed of six or seven whorls; the aperture is oblique, semielliptical, thin, and slightly reflected, with a broad internal band, distinctly visible from the outside; the umbilicus is narrow, but distinct. In very young shells the exterior is clothed with hairs, and in this state may be confounded with *H. hispida*, but is easily distinguished by the keel on the margin of the outer whorl, whilst in *H. hispida* the last whorl is rounded.

This snail inhabits gardens, hedge-banks, and under stones in the vicinity of dwellings; it is more abundant in limestone districts. It is common as far north as Yorkshire, and is unknown in Scotland and in the North of Ireland.

HELIX HISPIDA—(*the Bristly Snail*) (Pl. VIII., fig. 75)—is an extremely common snail in woods, among moss and herbage, and under stones, in shady places. The shell is about a quarter of an inch in breadth and about the same in height, of a dark yellowish-brown, transversely striated; the epidermis is clothed with crowded, fine, white, and recurved hairs. The umbilicus is small, narrow, but deep.

It varies in colour and in the elevation of the spire, but the thick yellowish-white foot of the animal affords a good distinction between it and the following species :—

HELIX CONCINNA—(*the Neat Snail*) (Pl. VIII., fig. 77)—is closely related to the last, and by some regarded as a variety of that species. The shell however is rather larger and less globose; the umbilicus is wider; the hairs are more scattered and readily fall off, and the shell thus often presents a smooth surface. The darker colour of the animal, the narrower and less fleshy foot, are good characters by which this species may be separated from *H. hispida*. Both species, more frequently than otherwise, have a white spiral

K

band in the last whorl, as in *H. rufescens.* The present species differs from the *Rufous Snail* in its smaller shell and in its more rounded and compact whorls, though equally numerous.

These three species are found together.

H. concinna has as wide a range as *H. hispida*, but is less frequent; in Ireland I have found the former in more exposed situations, about rocks upon the hill-slopes, than in which *H. hispida* is usually met with.

The number of teeth on the lingual ribbon approaches to that of *H. caperata;* there are a hundred transverse rows of fifty-one teeth.

HELIX SERICEA—(*the Silky Snail*) (Pl. VIII., fig. 65)—so called from the long and very fine white downy hairs which thickly cover the shell; when these are worn off, the surface presents a minutely granulated appearance; from which latter character Mr. Alder gave it the name of *H. granulata.*

The shell is conical, more globose than that of any of its allies, and is less than a quarter of an inch in diameter and as much high; thin, of a greyish-white; whorls very convex, six in number; the umbilical aperture is extremely small, which alone is sufficient to distinguish it from its congeners or any of their varieties.

This species is rare and local; in England it is chiefly confined to the South and West; it occurs in Scotland, and has not yet been found in Ireland. It is distributed throughout the temperate parts of Europe.

It lives in moist woods, damp places on the banks of streams, among the grass and rushes or under the leaves of *Petasites vulgaris.*

HELIX· FUSCA — (*the Brown Snail*) (Pl. VII., fig. 50).—The shell of this species is· of a glossy amber-colour, and is especially characterized by its strong, irregular, transverse wrinkles, and its extreme thinness and fragility. It has a minute umbilicus, like *H. sericea,* but the spire is more depressed, and the last whorl proportionately large. The height is a quarter of an inch, the breadth three-eighths.

In the northern parts of Great Britain this snail is common, in damp shady places and wooded mountain glens; on the fallen leaves of trees in the autumn, and in the summer upon the young trees of the sycamore and alder. It is a hardy species; for in the damp woods in the neighbourhood of Belfast I have frequently collected it in great numbers, during the winter months, gliding rapidly over the leaves of the wood-rush (*Luzula sylvatica*), to which it is very partial; it has occurred to me under similar circumstances in the glens of the lake districts of Scotland. It is very rare in the South of England; and on the Continent has hitherto only been found near

K 2

the sea at Boulogne and on the west coast of France.

HELIX REVELATA—(Pl. VIII., fig. 72).—The specific term signifies "discovered;" the vulgar name by which it is known is the "*Green Snail*," on account of its peculiar colour. The shell is subglobose, about a quarter of an inch in diameter, very thin, nearly transparent, green, wrinkled in the lines of growth; the umbilicus is small and narrow; in the living state the epidermis of the shell is provided with short rigid hairs, sparsely distributed.

H. revelata is one of the rarest of British snails, and was added to our fauna in 1841, by Mr. Bellamy, who found it near Mevagissey, between Falmouth and Plymouth. It occurs at Pendennis, near Falmouth; Whitesand Cliffs, near the roots or under the foliage of plants of recumbent growth; at Stanton-on-the-Wolds, Notts, in woods. It is procured under stones on the open downs in Devon and Cornwall, but in Guernsey in shady places among nettles. It is found in the South-west of France and in Portugal.

Mr. J. G. Jeffreys writes — "In winter and dry weather it buries itself rather deep in the earth, and must be looked for by pulling up tufts of grass and large stones which are sunk in the ground, as well as by searching among the roots of shrubs and furze-bushes."

HELIX LAMELLATA—(*the Plated Snail*) (Pl. VII., fig. 51)—is a characteristic northern shell. It inhabits woods, on decaying leaves of *Luzula* and fronds of *Lastrea*, &c., and about rocks near running water. It was first discovered near Scarborough, and is now known throughout the North of England, the North and West of Scotland, and the North of Ireland. Until recently, this species was peculiar to North Britain, but it has been found in North Germany and in Sweden.

This beautiful conical globose shell is only one-tenth of an inch high and broad, of greyish colour; and in certain lights it exhibits a satiny appearance, which is due to the action of the rays of light upon the fine, sharply-cut striæ which cover its surface.

HELIX ACULEATA—(*the Prickly Snail*) (Pl. VII., fig. 48).—This, also, is a minute species, and differs especially from the last in the epidermis of the shell being raised into from twenty to thirty plaits, which rise in the middle of each whorl to a sharp point. Fresh specimens are exquisitely beautiful objects, exhibiting the appearance of a coronet of bristles encircling each whorl.

This species is so minute, and its colour so closely resembles that of the dead leaves upon which it is usually found, that it is detected with difficulty, and it is advisable to lift the leaves and turn them over in the hand to find it. In Gloucestershire it is found on the under sides of the leaves of the hazel; it is occasionally seen on liver-worts (*Jungermanniæ*). *H. aculeata* is distributed throughout Britain and Europe.

HELIX POMATIA—(*the Apple Snail*) (Pl. VIII., fig. 73).—This snail is commonly regarded as the one which was held in so great repute by the epicures of ancient Greece and Rome; but this is not the fact, for a larger species replaces *H. pomatia* in Southern Europe. In the North of France and in Switzerland the Apple Snail, however, is a much-prized mollusk as an article of diet.

The shell of this species, the largest of our British snails, is globular, thick, and strong, of a yellowish-white, with spiral bands of brown; it is as much as two inches in breadth and height; the whorls are five in number, the last one extremely large and inflated.

This, the largest snail, possesses the greatest number of teeth among the *Helicidæ*, and they are only exceeded in number by those of the *Limaces*; the number is 21,140, contained in 140 rows of 151 each. The jaw (fig. 21) is strongly arched, with a moderate number of

Fig. 21.—Jaw of *H. pomatia.*

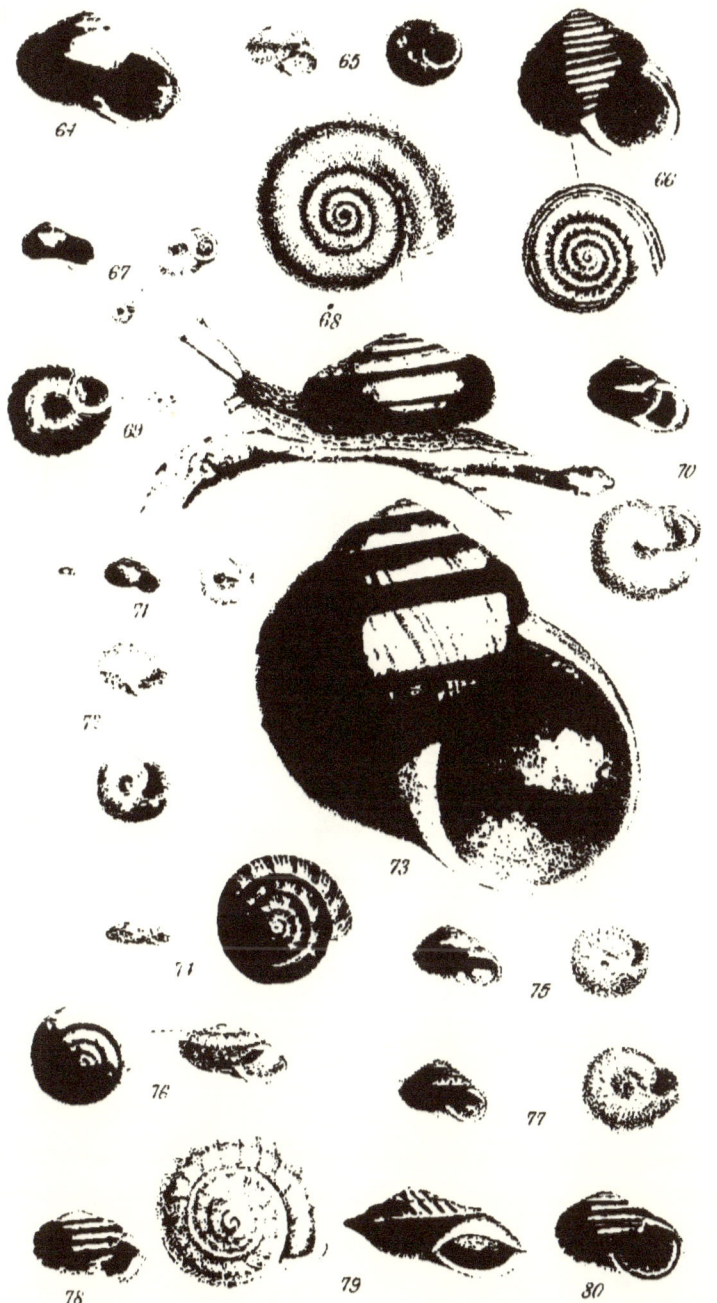

Plate VIII

64

65

66

67

68

69

70

71

72

73

74

75

76

77

78

79

80

prominent ribs, which form strong teeth on the free margin.

H. pomatia is to be met with on the borders of copses and woods on a calcareous soil. It is found at Sevenoaks, in Kent; Croydon, Reigate, and Dorking, in Surrey; in Hertfordshire, Oxfordshire, and Wilts; it is common on the Cotswold range. In early spring these snails unite for propagation. The eggs are globular, and covered with a white opaque skin, and are about the size of small peas; these are laid in a kind of nest, made in the loose earth, in the months of June and July. The eggs are hatched in twenty to thirty days, according to the season and temperature; when first excluded, the young live solely on the egg-cases; at the end of the year they are about the size of *Helix hispida*, and arrive at maturity in a little more than a year.

The Apple Snail, on the arrival of the period of hybernation, constructs, by the aid of its large muscular foot, and a very glutinous secretion, a hole in the ground, just large enough to receive the shell; this it lines with dead leaves, retires to its hybernaculum, and closes the aperture of the shell with a solid calcareous plate, secreted and formed by the mantle; it then withdraws considerably within the shell, and the more effectually to exclude the cold air, forms several but much thinner epiphragms, behind which it rests in a torpid state during the winter; thus it remains unconscious of what is going on around it—sleeping through the winter months, until the genial showers of April call it forth. Its specific name *pomatia* is derived from the Greek *poma*, an operculum, from the thick calcareous epiphragm it forms.

This snail has been the object of numerous experiments, with the view of ascertaining the extent of the remedial power among land mollusks. The Abbé Spallanzani cut off the tentacles, which were reproduced even to the eyes at the end of two months; not content with subjecting the creature to such torture, he tested the reparative power in a greater degree, by removing the entire head, which was reproduced to perfection. The snails thus experimented upon, retired immediately into their shells, and there remained weeks or months, outwardly in a state of quiescence, but internally the wonderful power of reproduction was silently at work until the end was attained.

The *Helices* diminish in size with their range in elevation; but *H. pomatia*, on the other hand, increases in size according to the altitude attained. It is found on the Vaudois Alps, up to the very verge of the forests, 5,850 feet above the level of the sea.

Some writers have asserted that this species has no claim to rank as indigenous to this country, but that it was introduced either as an article of food, or for medicinal purposes.

HELIX ARBUSTORUM (Pl. VII., fig. 62), as the specific name implies, the "*Shrub Snail*," is a tenant of our woods and groves, preferring moist situations, but more frequently its habitat is among the willows and reeds of our ditch sides and river banks.

The shell of *H. arbustorum* is certainly handsome; it is globular, about three-fourths of an inch in diameter, generally brown, marbled with yellowish spots, and having a single blackish band winding round the middle of each whorl. The animal is covered with tubercles, and is of a greenish-black colour, of a light grey beneath the foot; the tentacles are short and black, with very globular extremities.

The shell presents numerous variations, both in form, and more especially in colour. Some are very thin and almost transparent, of a dark colour, with or without the band; in others the shells are variegated, with a brown band, or more strongly marked with a black one; whilst in others the spire is much more prominent.

The Shrub Snail is distributed over the greater part of Europe; in Great Britain it is somewhat localized, though it has a place in most local .

lists. This species reaches a higher elevation than any other, being found high up on mountain-sides; in the Alps it attains to the region of perpetual snow. At this great altitude the shell is smaller, and the spire more elevated, and is the variety *alpina* (Pl. VII., fig. 62*a*).

HELIX PULCHELLA—(*the Pretty or White Snail*) (Pl. VIII., fig. 67)—is another of the little-isms of molluscan life. The animal is milk-white, and its black eyes contrast strongly with the transparency of the upper tentacles. The shell partakes of the colour of the animal, is rather opaque and depressed in form; there are three and a half rounded whorls, the last one exceeding the rest of the shell in size: the circular aperture has a very thick and strongly reflected margin, forming a complete peristome; the umbilicus is large and deep; the diameter is a tenth of an inch.

Fig. 22. Jaw of
H. pulchella.

The accompanying figure represents the striated horny jaw of this little beauty. The number of teeth far exceeds in number those of *Helicella cellaria*, which possesses a shell many times the size of this minute species; the dental formula is $\frac{15 \cdot 1 \cdot 15}{60} = 1860$.

It is widely distributed throughout Britain and Europe, and ranges to Siberia, and is found in Madeira and the Azores.

This species is usually regarded as an inhabitant of North America, but the species there is clearly distinct from the European *H. pulchella;* the American *H. minuta* of Say is clearly indigenous, for it is widely and abundantly distributed, and in regions remote from the sea, throughout North America.

It frequents walls, under stones, and among the short herbage of downs.

A variety—*H. pulchella* β. *costata* (Pl. VIII., fig. 69)—has the shell furnished with elevated, transverse, and curved ridges, and is stated to be peculiar to marshy and damp situations. In this I do not acquiesce, for I have found both living together in dry places, as on the walls of Hastings Castle, under stones on the Chalk Downs of Sussex, and at Bristol; and in damp and low situations, as among the osier beds bordering the banks of the river Thames, both the smooth form and costated variety occur. In a parcel of shells of this species from any of these localities, specimens showing the transition from the ridged variety to the smooth form are not rare.

The variety *costata* should be regarded as the normal form, as the ribless condition results from the disappearance of the costæ upon the shell, which is due to the occasional wearing away by age, just as in the case of *H. aculeata*, which is sometimes found without the longitudinal plates which generally cover the shell.

HELIX LAPICIDA—(*the Variegated Rock Snail*) (Pl. VIII., fig. 79)—the technical name, signifying "a stone-cutter," is very inappropriate, and was given to this species by the great Linnæus, from an erroneous idea that it ate or excavated limestones.

The shell is depressed, lens-shaped, convex above and below, with a sharp keel on its outer circumference; the aperture is longitudinally oval and angular; the white and reflected peristome is united all round; the edge is acute but not thickened. The colour of the shell resembles that of *H. rotundata*, is yellowish-red, irregularly streaked across the whorls with reddish-brown; the surface is also striated with closely-set lines of growth; the umbilicus is large. The dental formula is $\frac{4\,0\cdot1\cdot4\,0}{1\,5\,0}$.

This snail is truly a woodland species, and is confined to the central and southern counties of England; it is found as far north as Brockerdale near Pontefract. It has a wide range in Europe.

It has been supposed to be restricted to limestone tracts, but I have found it very general in the woods of the Wealden district, where the rocks are especially characterized by the absence of the calcareous element. In Gloucestershire, this snail occurs in great plenty on the trunks of beech trees having a southern aspect.

HELIX OBVOLUTA—(*the Cheese Snail*) (Pl. VII., fig. 49)—the aperture of the shell of this species is rather curious, and alone is sufficient to distinguish it; it is obliquely triangular, with a toothlike protuberance. The shell is nearly circular, flatabove, with the spire slightly sunk, compressed below, and with a large umbilicus; the whorls, six in number, are closelywrapped together, cylindrical, compressed from side to side, and gradually increasing in size; the last one is dilated towards the mouth. Young shells want the triangular mouth and reflected lip.

The colour of the shell is reddish, with the epidermis raised into curved ridges, and clothed with short stiff brown hairs. The dental formula is $\frac{4\ 5 \cdot 1 \cdot 4\ 5}{1\ 7\ 0}$.

The principal locality for this shell is Ditcham Wood, near Buriton, Hampshire; it is also found at Uppark and Stoner Hill, in the same county. In Ditcham Wood it occurs abundantly, and hybernates at the base of hazel trees; the epiphragm is thick and of a chalky-white colour.

HELIX ERICETORUM—(*the Heath Snail*) (Pl. VIII., fig. 68).—The shell of this species is very elegant, of a circular flattened form, with an exceedingly large umbilicus and a nearly circular mouth. These characters will enable one readily to separate it from *H. virgata,* and the other banded snails. The shell is composed of six whorls, usually of a white colour, with a broad band around the middle of the whorl, with from two to six narrower ones below.

The diameter of the shell is one inch. The dental formula is $\frac{3.0 \cdot 1 \cdot 3.0}{1 \cdot 1 \cdot 5}$.

The animal is very sluggish in its movements, timid, and retreating within its shell on the slightest touch. Excessive rains destroy great numbers of them, as I have observed on the Cotswold Hills.

It is an abundant species on the chalk and oolitic hills of England, and is pretty generally diffused throughout Ireland and Scotland.

It has a predilection for limestone soils, though not confined to them, for many of the sand dunes around our coasts claim it.

HELIX ROTUNDATA—(*the Radiated Snail*) (Pl. VIII., fig. 74)—is one of our common *Helices,* and is provided with not an unhandsome shell, which is flattish and circular; the whorls are six in number, slightly convex above, more compressed below; the last one is slightly angular; the umbilicus is very large, exposing the interior of all the whorls; the colour is reddish-brown, marked in a radiating manner with spots of brown and yellowish-grey; it is sometimes found transparent and colourless. Another variety, *H. Turtoni,* has the spire quite flattened. The diameter of the shell is one-third of an inch.

This snail inhabits a great variety of situations, —beneath stones in damp woods, on rocks, among fallen leaves, and shows a predilection for decaying wood.

HELIX RUPESTRIS—(*the Wall Snail*) (Pl. VII., fig. 46)—is one of our minute species, passing its days between the bricks and stones at the tops of old walls and ruins of castles, on the rocks, and under *débris* on hill-sides, usually in dry, lofty, and exposed situations, and attaches itself more markedly to limestone rock, though I have found it on sandstones in the North of Ireland; on the quartzose conglomerate of Bristol; but certainly very abundantly on the limestone of the oolitic rocks of the West of England, among the *débris* of the quarries and on the bare rock surfaces. It is rare in Ireland.

The shell is somewhat conical, of a blackish-brown colour, slightly glossy, marked transversely with strong, oblique curved striæ; the whorls are five in number, rounded, separated from one another by a deep suture; the aperture is nearly circular; umbilicus very large; the diameter of the shell is one-tenth of an inch. A well-known synonym for this species is *H. umbilicatus*, suggested by the open umbilicus, which so markedly characterizes it.

The spire in old specimens is whitish, by exposure. The snail in crawling carries its shell upright, and not inclined to one side, like the majority of the *Helices*. A peculiarity possessed by this snail is that of retaining the eggs in the interior of the shell (ovoviviparous) until they are hatched. Mr. J. G. Jeffreys has found the young under such circumstances, with a whorl and a half formed.

HELIX PYGMÆA—(*the Pigmy Snail*) (Pl. VIII., fig. 71).—This beautiful tiny gem, so interesting from its minuteness, is no bigger than the head of a good-sized pin; and on account of its minute size, it is difficult to find; but the much-prized treasure is within the reach of all, and will be found by him who searches properly for it; for it is widely diffused throughout Britain. Firstly, then, to describe the object of our search, and then to direct attention to where it is likely to occur.

The shell is nearly circular, with four convex whorls, of a pale brown colour, semi-transparent, and having a silky lustre, slightly striated; aperture crescent-shaped; umbilicus large.

It differs from *H. rupestris*, its closest ally, in its much smaller size, finer texture and ornamentation, lighter colour, fewer whorls, more depressed spire, and more open umbilicus.

It is partial to shade and moisture, under

stones, and at the roots of grass; but more frequently on dead leaves in woods and plantations.
Moquin-Tandon, in his " Natural History of
the Land and Fresh-water Mollusks of France,"
writes of this pigmy, that it is timid and irritable, avoids the bright sunlight, retires within
its shell at the slightest touch; and that the
first part of the body protruded from the shell
is the hinder portion of the foot.

GEOLOGICAL DISTRIBUTION OF HELIX.—One
of the most ancient of the *Helices* that has survived through a long space of time—from the
deposition of the Upper Eocene, at the close of
which period in the Isle of Wight it became
extinct—to the present day, is *H. labyrinthica*;
for it has been driven from the hemisphere in
which it first appeared to North America, where
it is now a widely-spread species.

Of the living British species, the following
are found fossilized in the Upper Tertiaries at
Copford, Grays, &c., Essex :—*H. hortensis, H.
nemoralis, H. arbustorum, H. hispida, H. concinna, H. pulchella, H. fusca, H. rufescens,
H. aculeata, H. lamellata, H. sericea, H. lapicida, H. virgata,* and *H. rotundata,* associated
with *H. fruticum, H. incarnata,* and *H. ruderata,*
which, though distributed throughout Northern
and Southern Europe, ceased to exist in Great
Britain at the close of the period of the deposi

tion of the Pleistocene fresh-water marls of Essex, &c. With them is also *Hydrobia marginata*, which, though not now found living in Britain, is repelled to Switzerland and Southern France. *H. hispida* and *H. arbustorum* lived during the Mammiliferous Crag epoch; and *H. pulchella* and the extinct *H. rysa* as early as that of the Red Crag. *H. pomatia* is fossilized in the bone-caves of Belgium, and *H. aspersa* in those of Gibraltar; and in the Uppermost Tertiaries at Newbury. The majority of the species occur in the sub-aërial deposits of the districts which they now inhabit.

Genus Bulimus.

The animal of *Bulimus* presents no real differences from that of *Helix;* the body is elongated, the tentacles are rather shorter, and the dentition is Helicine : the transverse rows extend in a straight line to about half their breadth, and then in a slight curve to the margin; the teeth are minute, and have a central, bluntly conical point, flanked on each side by a very much smaller but similar one. The shell is oblong, or turreted; the peristome is thin, or reflected. There are only three British species, belonging to two sections—*B. acutus*, with a turreted shell and a simple peristome; *B. montanus* and *B.*

obscurus, with an oblong shell and a reflected peristome.

Bulimus has persisted since the period of the Bembridge Limestone of the Upper Eocene. *B. montanus* and *B. obscurus* are both fossils of the Pleistocene marls; the former at Clacton and Orton, the latter at Copford.

Many of the pulmoniferous snails now rare in this country were formerly abundant, and had a wider geographical range than at present; *e. g.*, *Bulimus montanus, Clausilia biplicata, C. Rolphii, Pupa substriata, Vertigo minutissima, V. angustior, Helix lamellata*, and *Succinea oblonga*.

BULIMUS ACUTUS — (*the Banded Twist Shell*) (Pl. IX., fig. 83)—is a very conspicuous shell, from the contrast of colours presented by it, thus differing from its congeners, which have a uniformly coloured shell. The shell is cylindrical, acute, with eight or nine rounded whorls, gradually increasing in size; the aperture is small, and the outer lip is thin and plain, not reflected, as in the majority of the *Helicidæ*; it rarely exceeds half an inch in length. The colour is generally yellowish-white, with bands of reddish-brown to black. The dental formula is $\frac{16 \cdot 1 \cdot 13}{100}$.

It is a somewhat local species, and inhabits the calcareous downs and the sandy pastures and dunes on the sea-coast, especially in the South and West of England, North and East of Ireland,

and the west of Scotland.   It lives in company
with *Helix virgata* and *H. caperata*, which it exceeds in abundance.   In the marshy grass lands
of the alluvial plains of Pett and Pevensey
Levels, in Sussex, *B. acutus* does not occur ; but
its usual associates literally carpet the swards
in many parts ; on the other hand, the two
Helices may be absent, and *B. acutus* is the sole
molluscan tenant of the almost barren sandy
wastes skirting, here and there, our coasts.

BULIMUS MONTANUS—(*the Mountain Twist Shell*)
(Pl. IX., fig. 81).—The shell of this species is
nearly three-fourths of an inch in length, conical, oblong, semi-transparent, glossy, of a light
reddish-brown colour, marked with spiral, close-
set, fine, undulating striæ.   The spire consists of
seven whorls ; the aperture is about one-fourth
of an inch wide ; the peristome is reflected.

It occurs in great abundance from April to
September, associated with *B. obscurus, Balea
fragilis, Clausalia laminata*, and *Helix lapicida*,
upon the large beech-trees in the woods on the
oolitic hills of Gloucestershire.   It prefers a
southern aspect, and ascends the trunks of trees
to heights which render it undistinguishable.
The beech is an especial favourite with snails,
more so than any other tree : its smooth bark is
what they delight in ; and after showers the
trunks may be seen studded with them ; the

probable explanation is, that this tree is resorted to by the snails for the purpose of feeding upon the minute parasitic vegetation which clothes it. The supposed scarcity of this snail, and some others, in localities where they are in reality most abundant, is due to this peculiar habit of ascending trees during the summer months; for at this season only dead shells will reward a search among the herbage at the bases of the trees.

B. montanus is readily to be distinguished from *B. obscurus*, which accompanies it, by its superior size and somewhat polished appearance; *B. obscurus*, in all stages, is covered with a dirty incrustation.

This species is recorded from Wiltshire and Hampshire, and in Suffolk near Bury St. Edmund's; it is thus local, but plentiful where it occurs.

The specific name, *montanus*, implies that its usual habitat is in elevated situations, and in such it is only known in Central Europe.

BULIMUS OBSCURUS — (*the Dull Twist Shell*) (Pl. IX., fig. 82).—This species differs from *B. montanus* chiefly in its smaller size, for the shell is about half an inch in length; and in the white reflected margin of the aperture. Albinos have occurred.

The animal is of a greyish-brown, or dark brown above; the foot is of a lighter colour;

when viewed under a lens, darker spots and markings are seen arranged in a beautiful pattern. The tentacles are cylindrical, granulated, and distinctly club-shaped. The dental formula is $\frac{27 \cdot 1 \cdot 27}{140}$.

B. obscurus is distributed throughout Britain, but not generally frequent; it is very local in Ireland; its habitats are under stones in woods, on rocks, and more frequently, when of course it is not hybernating, upon the trunks of trees. This little snail, in all stages of growth, covers itself with a coating adapted to the different situations in which it is found, rendering its detection difficult. "If its abode," according to Mr. Sheppard, " be upon the trunk of a tree covered with lichens, then is the epidermis so constructed as to cause the shell to resemble a little knot on the bark, covered with such substances. If on a smooth tree, from whose bark issue small sessile buds, as is frequently the case, it will pass off very well for one of them; and on a dry bank, or the lower part of the body of a tree splashed with mud, its appearance will be that of a little misshapen pointed piece of dirt."

GENUS ZUA.

This genus is distinguished from *Bulimus* by the glossy transparent shell, and the thickened but not reflected lip. The animal resembles that of *Bulimus*. The genus contains only one British species—

ZUA LUBRICA—(*the Common Varnished Shell*) (Pl. IX., fig. 84).—The shell is glossy, of a brown or yellowish colour, sometimes greenish-white; about one-fourth of an inch long, usually of an oblong, cylindrical shape, but subject to some variation in shape and colour.

It is common and generally distributed; inhabits woods, among decaying leaves and wood, at the roots of plants, and on mossy banks and swards. It is a favourite food of the starling. It is a fossil of the Newer Tertiaries of Grays, Clacton, Copford, &c.

A North American species, *Zua lubricoidea* (Stimpson), has been unhesitatingly referred to the common European species by all conchological writers, with the exception of two— Stimpson, who named the species as above, deeming it impossible that an introduced species could have spread so generally over the American Continent; and Morse, who has shown, during the past year, that certain marked and constant characters plainly indicate the distinctness of the species. Slight differences in colour, size, and number of whorls may be pointed out, as also differences in the lingual dentition; that of *Z. lubrica* being $\frac{20 \cdot 1 \cdot 20}{80}$; of the American species,

$\frac{21 \cdot 1 \cdot 21}{9 \, 0}$. The central tooth in each is small : that of *Z. lubrica* is simple, whereas that of *Z. lubricoidea* has a minute denticle on each side.

· GENUS AZECA.

Azeca and *Zua* are separated from *Bulimus* by artificial characters; for there are no structural differences between the animals of these three genera. The shell of *Azeca* in form and colour is like that of *Zua*, and is equally polished; but the aperture is furnished with folds or teeth, of which there are usually three. There is only one British species—

AZECA TRIDENS — (*the Glossy Trident Shell*) (Pl. IX., fig. 85).—This snail is rare and sparingly distributed throughout England, and is more frequently met with on the chalky and oolitic soils of Suffolk, Essex, Kent, Surrey, Gloucestershire, &c.; inhabiting the moss and dead leaves in moist woods, congregated in little parties of six to nine. It occurs in the Newer Tertiary deposits of Copford and Clacton.

GENUS PUPA (*Chrysalis Snails*).

The animal is furnished with a short foot, acute behind; the tentacles are short, especially the lower ones; in the SUB-GENUS VERTIGO the inferior tentacles are obsolete.

The Chrysalis Snails, or *Pupæ*, are so named from the fancied resemblance of their shells to an insect in the second stage of its metamorphism—that is, to a chrysalid; also to dolls or puppets.

The shell is cylindrical or oblong, with many narrow whorls, minutely umbilicated; the aperture is oval or lunate, generally toothed within; the peristome is incomplete, thickened, and reflected.

The *Pupæ* are widely distributed on the globe; the majority of them inhabit South-eastern Europe. Four species are indigenous to this country and, excepting *P. secale*, are found fossilized in the Newer Tertiaries of the East of England. *Pupa* is the most ancient genus of the land mollusca, the earliest known species of which is *P. vetusta*, of the Coal-measures of Nova Scotia. Two species are extinct in the Upper Eocene of the Isle of Wight. The species now inhabiting Britain may be characterized as follows :—

1. { One tooth, or edentulous 2
   { Aperture with many teeth 3

2. { Tooth in the upper angle of the outer lip,—*P. umbilicata*
   { Peristome with external rib, tooth central,—*P. muscorum*

3. { Shell ventricose, shining, 5-toothed ... *P. anglica*
   { Shell cylindrical, dull, 8-toothed ... ... *P. secale*

PUPA UMBILICATA—(*the Umbilicated Chrysalis*

Shell) (Pl. IX., fig. 97)—is one of the most common of the land mollusca throughout the British isles. It frequents old ivied walls, about rocks, under stones, among moss and herbage and dead leaves; from the sea-shore to great elevations.

The shell is oblong, cylindrical, glossy, yellowish-brown or dark horn-colour, composed of six rounded whorls, which are faintly and irregularly striated in the line of growth; the aperture is subangular; the lip is thickened and much reflected, and white or pale yellowish-grey on the inside; a single tooth occupies the angle formed by the junction of the outer lip; there is a small and narrow umbilicus; the length of the shell is two-twelfths of an inch, and the breadth about half. It is subject to variation in form and colour: some want the tooth; specimens with two teeth have occurred to collectors; others have the shell whitish or colourless.

This species is ovoviviparous.

PUPA MUSCORUM—(*the Margined Chrysalis Shell*) (Pl. IX., fig. 98)—is very closely allied to *P. umbilicata*, but differs from it in being more cylindrical, with the last whorl smaller; the mouth is more oval, less triangular, and the tooth is placed centrally and considerably within the aperture, but is, however, often absent. It is more especially to be distinguished by the margin of the aperture being expanded, reflected, and strengthened by a thick white external rib; from which latter character it has received the name of *P. marginata.* Individuals living in moist and grassy places are light brown, and more or less glossy and transparent; those much exposed to the weather are often grey or whitish and opaque. This is equally the case with many other glossy shells.

P. badia of Adams, a North American snail, is considered by some European authors to be identical with this species, and it, like its ally, is ovoviviparous.

The species is common throughout Britain; it is partial to dunes and sandy pastures, among grass and roots of *Psamma arenaria*, bordering the sea-coast, and among the rejectamenta of our tidal rivers; inland it occurs on rocks, under stones, on walls, and among moss.

PUPA ANGLICA—(*the English Chrysalis Shell*) (Pl. IX., fig. 99).—This species was added to our molluscan fauna in 1822, by Mr. Bean, and was considered peculiar to England when described by Ferussac; hence its trivial name. It is found throughout the northern counties of England, the West of Scotland, and all Ireland; it is by no means general, or, except in particular spots, plentiful.

Though a British species of a northern type,

it is, however, found in Algeria, and in the neighbourhood of Oporto, in Portugal.

The shell is sub-cylindrical, shining, and varying in colour from pale greyish- to a deep reddishbrown, or rarely white; the whorls are six; the aperture is triangular, and rounded below, with five folds; the margin of the aperture and the folds are generally of the colour of the shell, but sometimes white.

It frequents dead leaves and moss in moist woods, and generally in company with *Helix lamellata,* with which it is also associated in a fossil state, in the newer Pleiocene deposits of Copford, in Essex. The Rev. J. Dalton observes, that "I have been told that this species never ascends trees, but I took no less than fifty-three specimens in one day from the trunk of a young ash-tree, covered with woodbine, in Hackfall, Ripon. This was after long-continued rain. In dry weather it is very seldom found; and until the above-mentioned day I believed it to be a very rare species."

Mr. J. G. Jeffreys writes of the habits of this snail, that "this is a shy little creature, although tolerably active when inclined to make its appearance. It has a singular habit of withdrawing slowly one of its eyes, which rolls backwards like a little ball until it reaches the neck, while the tentacle which supports it remains extended to its full length. This I have observed being done when there was no obstacle in the way. It also retracts occasionally, and apparently without any reason, one of its horns and not the other. It does not appear to be ovoviviparous, like *P. umbilicata.*"

PUPA SECALE—(*the Juniper Chrysalis Shell*) (Pl. IX., fig. 96).—The shell is larger and more tapering than that of any other British *Pupa*; is a quarter of an inch or more in length, cylindrical in form, and composed of eight or nine rounded and gradually increasing whorls, obliquely striated in the line of growth; the colour is a light brown; the aperture is much contracted by the seven laminar folds—two, and sometimes three, are on the pillar, two occupy the pillar lip, and four the outer lip; the teeth on the outer lip are distinctly visible on the exterior of the shell as white bands. The number of rows, and number of teeth in a row, composing the palatal membrane of *P. secale*, are thus—100 rows, 41 in a row; total, 4,100.

This species is local, and chiefly confined to the limestone tracts of the South and West of England. On the oolitic hills it is very abundant, attached to stones or to the bare rock surface by a thin pellicle during the daytime: from the accidental adhesion of earthy matter to the shell, especially of the young, it may escape notice. The animal is sluggish, and is not frequently to be seen stirring about.

GENUS VERTIGO (*Whorl Snails*).

The animal differs from that of *Pupa* in being destitute of the lower pair of tentacles. The shell is minute, sometimes sinistral; the peristome is thinner than in *Pupa*. Of the nine species inhabiting this country, *V. Moulinsiana* is the only one not known in a fossilized state.

The species may be distinguished as follows :—

1. { Shell dextral 2
   { Shell sinistral 8

2. { Aperture edentulous 3
   { Aperture toothed 4

. 3. { Shell small, slightly striated ... ... *V. edentula*
     { Shell minute, strongly striated ... *V. minutissima*

4. { Shell oval 5
   { Shell cylindrical 7

5. { Aperture 4-toothed 6
   { Aperture with many teeth, aperture contracted,—
   {   *V. antivertigo*

6. { Shell small ... ... *V. pygmœa*
   { Shell large ... ... *V. Moulinsiana*

7. { Shell subcylindrical, 4-toothed ... ... *V. alpestris*
   { Shell inclined to fusiform, strongly striated,—
   {   *V. substriata*

8. { Aperture subquadrate, six to seven teeth,—*V. pusilla*
   { Aperture triangular, contracted, four to six teeth,—
   {   *V. angustior*

VERTIGO EDENTULA—(*the Toothless Whorl Shell*) (Pl. X., fig. 101).—The shell is dextral, cylindrical, with five or six rounded whorls, which are slightly transversely striated; the third whorl is the largest; the aperture is semicircular and toothless, with the peristome very slightly reflected; the colour is brown or horn, with the peristome paler; the length is one-tenth of an inch.

An elongated variety has seven or occasionally eight whorls, and attains the maximum length of one and a half lines.

The typical form is generally found under stones and on rocks; the variety inhabits moister places; both, however, occur in woods, on the fallen leaves of trees in the winter and autumn; in the summer frequenting the under fronds of *Aspidium filix-mas* and other ferns.

This elegant little mollusk presents a grotesque appearance when crawling, for the shell is carried in a singularly erect position.

VERTIGO MINUTISSIMA—(Pl. X., fig. 100).—As the specific name implies, this is a tiny shell, and is not a line in length; it is nearly cylindrical, with five rounded whorls, which increase suddenly to the third, and then continue nearly of the same size, ornamented with acute oblique transverse striations. It resembles *V. edentula* in the aperture and in the absence of teeth, but is distinguished from that species by its very minute size, and in the strongly striated surface of the shell. It occurs here and there in England and Scotland; it harbours under stones on hills, chiefly those that are limestone. In Scotland it occurs in Skye; Balmerino, Fifeshire; Arthur's Seat. In England, on magnesian limestone, Falcon Clints, near Sunderland; and near Pontefract, in Durham; Wakefield, and Went Vale, Yorkshire; Durdham Downs, Bristol; Sulworth, in Dorset; and on the Undercliff, in the Isle of Wight. Its minute size may account - for its apparent rarity. It is a continental species, and widely diffused.

VERTIGO PYGMÆA—(the *Pigmy Whorl Shell*) (Pl. IX., fig. 90).—The shell is oval, about one-tenth of an inch long, of a brown shining colour; the four or five whorls gradually increase in size; the aperture is dextral, with a slightly reflected margin, and provided usually with four teeth, one of which is central on the upper side or pillar.

This is one of the most widely distributed of the *Vertigos;* it may be easily procured under stones upon dry and elevated situations.

A thinner shell, and of a lighter colour than the typical form, is known to collectors; I have found it under stones on the shores of the Irish upland lakes, and in damp fields in England.

VERTIGO ALPESTRIS—(*the Alpine Whorl Shell*) (Pl. IX., fig. 88)—differs from the last species, and is regarded by many as a variety of it, in being more cylindrical, of a paler colour, slightly striated, and in the absence of any rib, either inside or outside, to the mouth.

Messrs. Forbes and Hanley say, " It may be taken in great numbers by laying a piece of old wood upon the grass at nightfall, and examining it in the morning."

It occurs in a few places in Cumberland, Lancashire, and Northumberland; at Over, Gloucester, and among moss on the canal banks at Sharpness (Mr. J. Jones); and is sparingly distributed in North and Central Europe.

VERTIGO ANTIVERTIGO—(*the Marsh Whorl Shell*) (Pl. X., fig. 103).—The shell of this species is dextral, and is not reversed, as in some others of the genus; it is of an oval form, thin, slightly polished, and of a brown colour; whorls five; the aperture is small, subtriangular, with a whitish margin, and provided with three unequal folds above on the pillar, and three on each side.

A very appropriate specific name given to this snail was *palustris*, as denoting that it was an inhabitant of marshy places, about the roots of plants; it is also to be met with under stones on the banks of streams and lakes, even in elevated situations. Though an inhabitant of

M

such places, the shell is always free from dirt and has a bright glossy lustre.

VERTIGO MOULINSIANA (Pl. X., fig. 105), named after M. des Moulins, a French conchologist, by the Abbé D. Dupuy. It is one of the most recent additions to our land shells. This acquisition to the British mollusca was made by Mr. J. G. Jeffreys in 1845, but not until the last few years was this discovery published. The only British locality is Ballinahinch, near Roundstone, co. Galway, where it inhabits under stones by the side of a small lake at the fore-mentioned place. It is local and rare in Central Europe. The affinities and differences here given of the shell of this species are quoted from the above-named author :—" The species differs from *V. antivertigo* in being larger, more ventricose, in the mouth and lip not being contracted, and especially in the number and position of the teeth, which never exceed four. From *V. pygmœa* by being twice the size and very much more ventricose. *V. Moulinsiana* resembles *V. antivertigo* in form, and *V. pygmœa* in the number of teeth. It is among the largest of our native species of *Vertigo*."

VERTIGO SUBSTRIATA — (*the Six-toothed Whorl Shell*) (Pl. X., fig. 104).—The shell of this species is somewhat fusiform, strongly striated transversely, and of a yellowish-horn colour; the aperture is furnished with from four to six folds —two or three on the pillar, and two or three on the outer lip. It is easily distinguished from the other *Vertigos* with dextral shells, by its form, the strong striæ, and in the number and position of the teeth.

It is a rare species, occurring chiefly in the North; it has a wide distribution, though rare, in Ireland; and has a limited range in Europe. It occurs among decaying leaves in glens, but more usually under stones on the banks of lakes, and at the roots of rushes. It is abundant in a fossil state in the Copford deposits.

VERTIGO PUSILLA — (*the Wry-necked Whorl Shell*) (Pl. X., fig. 102).—The shells of this and the following species are sinistral and spindle-shaped; that of *V. pusilla* possesses six or seven folds within the aperture, which is subquadrate.

It lives on old walls and dry banks, under stones, among leaves in woods, and is diffused throughout England, but is local and rare; it is very rare in Ireland, and has been found in only a few localities in the North-east and West. It is a North and Central European species.

VERTIGO ANGUSTIOR—(*the Narrow Whorl Shell*) (Pl. X., fig. 111).—The shell of this species differs from the last in its much smaller size, in being proportionately narrower, and in possessing only four to six teeth. The aperture is narrow and triangular, in consequence of the great contraction of its outer edge in the middle. It is found about the roots of grass in marshy places in a few localities :—Singleton, near Swansea; Tenby; rejectamenta of the river Avon, at Bristol; Battersea; in Ireland, at Miltown Malby, co. Clare; Connemara, Galway; and at Cork. It occurs in Central Europe.

Genus Balea.

The animal is bulimus-like; the lingual ribbon is furnished with 130 rows of teeth, each row containing 50. The shell is thin, slender, elongated, of many reversed whorls; the aperture is ovate, with the peristome thin, and sometimes furnished with an imperfect fold on the columella. The genus is intermediate between *Pupa* and *Clausilia*, but differs from the former in the shape of the aperture and the elongated spire, and from the latter in having no clausium.

This generic group contains only a few species, one of which is indigenous to this country:—

BALEA PERVERSA—(*the Fragile Moss Shell*) (Pl. IX., fig. 86).—The shell is oblong, slender, yellowish, transversely striated with seven or eight distinct whorls; the aperture is roundish, oval, and reversed; the peristome is thin, and a little reflected on the columella, where there may be observed, in full-grown shells, a tubercle-like tooth; the length is usually about a quarter of an inch. The shell varies in size, shape, and colour; greenish-white and transparent examples have been found. The dental formula is $\frac{20 \cdot 1 \cdot 20}{130}$.

This species is generally distributed throughout Britain. In moist weather, these snails may be seen in some numbers on the trunks of trees; in dry weather, sheltering beneath the loose bark, or in the hollows and crevices of the trunks. Other favourite haunts are among decaying wood and dead leaves, or lurking in moss, or even on the tops of old ivied walls.

It occurs in a fossil state at Grays, in Essex.

GENUS CLAUSILIA (*Close Snails*).

The animal, closely resembling that of *Bulimus*, has a short, broad, and obtuse foot; the upper tentacles are short and the lower ones very small (Pl. IX., fig. 94). The shell is fusiform, of many reversed whorls; the last one is smaller than the one before it; the aperture is elliptical or pear-shaped, united all round, and toothed. In addition to the contraction and folds of the shell for the protection of the snail within, there is added an elastic appendage termed the *clausium*, which is capable of closing the aperture. The *clausium* is situated at the distance of about half a whorl from the mouth, and may be seen in position by breaking off the outer part of the last whorl; it consists of a thin, spoon-shaped *shelly* plate attached to the folds of the columella by an elastic filament. When the animal comes out of the shell, the *clausium* is pushed against the columella; and the elasticity of its filament also admits of it closing the aperture on the snail withdrawing within the shell. The *clausium* is not secreted until the snail is about to complete its shell; and is not attached to the animal, but is merely an appendage to the mouth of the shell.

About 300 species of *Clausilæ* are known, the majority of which inhabit South-eastern Europe. *Clausila* is represented in the Upper Eocene of the Isle of Wight; and the four species at present living in England, also found fossilized in the newer Tertiary deposit of Essex, are as follows:—

Shell smooth, glossy... ... ...   *C. laminata*
 „ streaked, with raised lines.
 „   „   with two columella folds   ...   *C. biplicata*
 „   „   „ three „   „   ...   *C. rugosa*
 „   „   „ four or five ; very fusiform   *C. Rolphii*

CLAUSILIA BIPLICATA—(*the Folded Close Shell*) (Pl. IX., fig. 95)—is larger than any of its congeners. The shell is two-thirds and occasionally three-fourths of an inch in length, with about twelve whorls; it is slender and thin, of a reddish or greyish-brown colour, with raised white lines; there are two folds on the columella.

C. biplicata is very rare, and was first described as British by Montagu. It may be found in some abundance under the larger osiers bordering the banks of the river Thames about Hammersmith. In the winter it buries the front of the shell in the loose soil among the tufts of grass or at the base of the trees. It is also recorded from two localities in Wiltshire.

CLAUSILIA LAMINATA—(*the Laminated Close Shell*) (Pl. IX., fig. 87).—The shell is large, handsome, and at once distinguished by its polished appearance; it is usually semi-transparent, glossy, yellowish- or reddish-brown, and sometimes greenish-white and transparent. There are twelve whorls; the aperture is oval, with two folds, from which latter character it is known as *C. bidens*, one of them curved and situated on the middle of the columella-lip, and the other is straight and near the top of the aperture; in addition there are three or four folds deep within the aperture, which are visible from the outside, owing to the transparency of the shell. The shell attains a length of three-fourths of an inch, but it varies in size and colour. The dentition is thus :—Number of rows, 120 ; number of teeth in a row, 51 ; total, 6,120.

This elegant species is local, and chiefly confined to the southern counties in England, reaching the limit of its northern distribution in Hulne Woods, Alnwick; it is rare in Ireland. *C. laminata* is especially met with in woods on a limestone soil; it is gregarious on the trunks of beech and other trees, during the night and after rain.

The eggs of this snail are very large in proportion to the animal, and are deposited among decaying wood in the autumn, to the number of ten or twelve; the young appear at the end of twenty days, and do not attain the adult state until the end of the second year.

CLAUSILIA RUGOSA — (*the Rugose Close Shell*) (Pl. IX., fig. 91).—This species is also known under the names of *C. nigricans* and *C. perversa;* it is the commonest of the *Clausiliæ,* and lives on walls, about rocks, and under stones, and on the trunks of beech and ash in woods.

The shell is more or less fusiform or spindle-shaped, of about half an inch in length, and composed of nine or ten, and not unfrequently twelve or thirteen whorls; the colour varies from a very pale greyish-white to a deep reddish-brown; greenish-white specimens are of rare occurrence; the shell is streaked with lines of grey, and striated obscurely or prominently in different individuals. The peristome is thickened, detached

Plate IX.

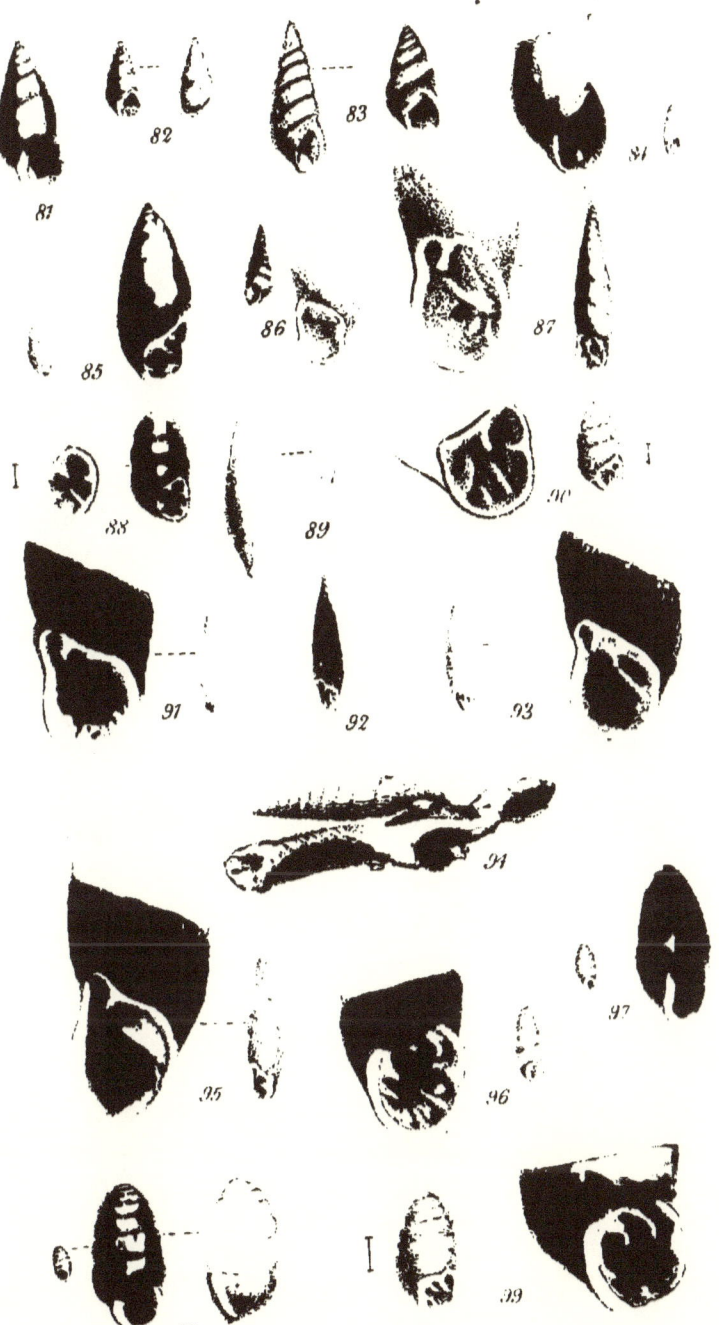

all round, more or less reflected, and whitish; it varies in form, being ovate, oblong, or subquadrate; the internal plaits are usually three in number, and all situated on the pillar. The *clausium* is curved, thin, with a thick revolute smooth margin. The dental formula is $\frac{20 \cdot 1 \cdot 20}{90}$.

The animal is very slender and elongated, and drags its shell in the same line as the foot and neck (see Pl. IX., fig. 14); for it is incapable of raising it, unless when about to repose, when the shell is inclined at an angle of about 70°.

A marked and persistent variety, *C. dubia* (Pl. IX., fig. 92), is characterized by its larger size and more spindle-shaped form; it is only recorded from the counties of York, Durham, and Northumberland.

CLAUSILIA ROLPHII (Pl. IX., fig. 93).— This species was named by Dr. Gray after Mr. Rolph, an English conchologist. It is easily distinguished from the other species of the genus by its more spindle-shaped shell, and in the presence of four or five folds, two of which are longer than the rest, within the aperture. The shell is half an inch to three-fifths in length, and one-seventh to one-eighth in breadth, of a slightly glossy reddish-brown, with regular transverse striations; there are ten and a half whorls; the aperture is subquadrate sinuous on the outer side; the margin is thick, white, and detached all round.

This rare species is found among dead leaves
and at the base of trees in woods in a few localities: in Kent — Ashford, Sevenoaks, Charlton
near London, Southborough, and Tunbridge
Wells; in Sussex—Hastings; in Hampshire—
Buriton, and Petersfield;· and in Gloucestershire
—Birdlip, Cooper's Hill, and Charlton, near
Cheltenham. Excepting in the Sussex localities,
where the soil is arenaceous, the rock formations
are chalk and oolite. It is not uncommon in
Central Europe.

A variety of the above species, but regarded
as having specific claims by Continental authors,
is *C. Mortilleti;* it has only been added to the
British list since 1856. It was discovered, by
Dr. S. P. Woodward, at the roots of ivy in
woods, on the chalk hills at Charing, Kent;
by Mr. Prentice, at Charlton-Kings, near Cheltenham; and by myself in damp shady places
among decaying leaves, in Coghurst Wood,
Hastings.

C. Rolphii occurs in each of the above districts,
which makes it the more probable that *C. Mortilleti* is but a variety of it. In *C. Rolphii* the
shell is usually more elongated, and the spire
more gradually decreasing in breadth towards
the apex; not ventricose, and suddenly narrow-
ing to the attenuated upper portion of the spire,
as in *C. Mortilleti*. It is lighter in colour, with

a fulvous tint rather than the purplish hue which pervades the latter ; *C. Mortilleti* has fewer teeth.

Genus Achatina (*Agate Shells*).

The shells of this genus are elongated, cylindrical, thin, glossy, and smooth ; the aperture is oval, and the outer lip thin and not reflected; the columella is twisted and truncated in front, that is, appearing as if cut off below. The species are very numerous, being about 150 in number, and especially inhabit tropical and subtropical forests and wastes. The majority of the agate shells are beautifully coloured.

The genus is represented by *A. costellata* in the Upper Eocene deposits of Bembridge, Isle of Wight.

The great African species are among the largest of the land mollusca, and attain a length of eight inches. The only British species is—

Achatina acicula—(*the Needle Agate Shell*) (Pl. IX., fig. 89)—and is a perfect Lilliputian among the snails with which it is generically allied; a pill-box, that may be carried in one's waistcoat pocket, is amply capacious for many of these pigmies, which rarely exceed one-sixth of an inch in length; whereas a collector among the giants of the race in tropical Africa and America requires a good-sized basket to bring home only a few specimens.

The animal of *Achatina acicula* is white and pellucid; the upper tentacles are long, but without eyes; the central tooth of the lingual ribbon is very small and pointed. The shell is very thin, slender, polished, and white, and, from its transparency, the dilatation and contraction of the respiratory cavity may be distinctly observed by the aid of a microscope, as irregular pulsations, reminding one of the action of the heart, for which it has been mistaken.

This handsome species is recorded, in the majority of local lists of land shells, as being found upon old walls or among the rejectamenta of rivers, but as dead shells; this appears to be accounted for by its subterranean habits, for its occurrence in a living state has been noticed when the soil or gravel has been overturned to a depth of some six or eight inches.

That such is not its sole habitat, I have had opportunities of satisfactorily determining; — thus, in many parts of the Cotswolds, this species has occurred to me in a living state, in bleak and dry situations, at an elevation of 500 to 1,000 feet, under stones, among the turf of these calcareous hills, or concealed deep in the fissures of the limestone rocks. I have even taken it among the acicular leaves of the larch and pine, in company with *Helicella pura, H. crystallina,* and *Vitrina;* this latter habitat is exceptional, because, "it is unusual to find molluscan life in such situations," for the presence of coniferous trees exerts a retarding influence on the growth and increase of land snails.

Its occurrence has been noticed by Mr. Bridgman, at Norwich, on a sunny bank near the Thorpe toll-bar, adhering to the roots of grass in the loose earth between the stones. "It was not, however," this gentleman writes, "at the roots of the grass, beneath the surface of the soil, but quite on the top, and also in the fine loose earth among the large flints, with which the bank is faced, and, in the first instance, adhering to the flint itself."

It is found sometimes abundantly amongst rotten wood.

It is inferred, because *A. acicula* usually lives underground, and has rarely been observed on the surface in a living state, that it feeds upon animal matter.

At the present time, this species has only been found here and there to the South of Yorkshire, and in the South and West of Ireland. It is distributed throughout Europe, and ranges into Asia Minor and Syria, and inhabits Algeria and Madeira.

Genus Succinea *(Amber Snails).*

The amber snails are so named because of the colour of the shells, which has some resemblance to that of *succinum* or amber; they have a large body with a broad foot, with the tentacles short

Fig. 23.—A transverse row of the lingual ribbon of *S. putris* (Lovèn).

and thick, as shown in Pl. VI, fig. 44. The lingual teeth are like those of *Helix;* in *S. putris,* the formula is $\frac{3\,2\cdot1\cdot3\,2}{5\,0}$, the central tooth differs only from the laterals in size: the teeth are three-lobed, the central is large (see fig. 23).

The shell is thin, oval or oblong, with a small spire and rapidly enlarging whorls, the aperture is large and obliquely oval. The oblong shape of the shell distinguishes it from those of the other members of the Family *Helicidæ,* but allies it to those of *Limnæidæ,* but separable from them by the absence of any oblique fold on the columella.

They all inhabit damp places, and though thriving on the stems of plants growing in the water, yet they rarely enter that element.

The most common and largest of the species is Succinea putris—*(the Common Amber Snail)*

(Pl. VI., fig 44; Pl. X., fig. 106).—The shell is oblong-oval, very thin, glossy, irregularly striated, and of an amber colour; the whorls are three in number; the spire is short; and the aperture ovate, two-thirds of the length of the shell, which is from a half to three-fourths of an inch.

This is an abundant species among herbage in marshy places, on the banks of ditches and pools; among sedges, grasses, and flags; in very hot weather, when the plants are desiccated, consequent upon the drying up of the water in the ditches, the amber snail descends to the lower parts of the stems of the plants upon which it feeds, whence it appears to follow the receding water at a certain distance.

S. putris is a fossil of the Mammaliferous Crag of Bramerton, and of the Pleistocene marls of Copford, &c.

SUCCINEA ELEGANS—(*the Elegant Amber Snail*) (Pl. X., fig. 107) — also known by the specific appellations of *Pfeifferi* and *gracilis*, is a closely allied species, or it may be but a variety of the last. The shell is more slender in shape, and with a longer and more pointed spire, and somewhat smaller in size; the shell, when containing the animal, appears of a greyish-blue, or bluish or greenish-black, for the body of the snail is black.

This species, though frequently associated with

S. putris, I find more generally on plants in bogs and maritime marshes; on plants and stones by mountain rills and lakes. It occurs with the last species in the Copford beds.

SUCCINEA OBLONGA—*(the Oblong Amber Snail)* (Pl. X., fig. 109) —is one of our rarities, and is markedly distinct from the two other species; it is always much smaller in size, with three or four distinctly separated whorls; the aperture is oval, and small in proportion to the size of the shell, being as long as the spire. The form of the shell of this species closely resembles that of *Limnæa truncatula,* but the absence of a reflected lip on the columella at once distinguishes it.

S. oblonga inhabits ditches near the coast, on sand-dunes near the sea, covering its shell with a viscous secretion, and in winter burying itself in the sand. There are two inland stations for it, both in Ireland : turf bogs, Finnoe, co. Tipperary; and damp woods, near Armagh : it is also found in woods in Central France, where it is nearly always met with slightly beneath the humus, which probably furnishes it with moisture, which it requires. It occurs near Swansea, Bideford, Berwick, Glasgow, and Cork. It is diffused throughout Europe, and is fossilized in the Pleistocene freshwater marls of Clacton, and in the Mammaliferous Crag at Bulcham and Maidstone.

FAMILY AURICULIDÆ.

This section of the Inoperculata contains only two British genera : *Carychium* and *Conovulus.* The former is truly terrestrial, whilst the Conovuli live on the mud at the mouths of rivers, or in the sea, and were long regarded as marine animals, but they are truly pulmoniferous.

The shell of *Carychium* is minute and ovate, with an oblong, three-toothed aperture ; the shell of *Conovulus* is also ovate, but the pillar presents two or three plaits.

GENUS CARYCHIUM.

, CARYCHIUM MINIMUM — (*the Minute Sedge Shell*) (Pl. XI., fig. 135).—This is an excedingly beautiful creature, and the smallest of British snails ; it is yellowish-white, provided with two conspicuous black eyes, near together at the base, and behind the tentacles. The dental formula is $\frac{1 \cdot 2 \cdot 1 \cdot 1 \cdot 2}{7}$.

The shell is very minute, scarcely one-tenth of an inch long, oblong, white, shining, and finely striated transversely ; there are five whorls ; the aperture is oval, with two teeth on the pillar, the margin is thickened and reflected, and presents a tooth projecting inwards in the middle of the outer lip.

N

The favourite abode of this minute species is among decaying leaves in woods, among herbage on mossy banks, and in moist places; it feeds on *Marchantia*. It is commonly distributed throughout Britain and Europe. In North America it is represented by the closely-allied *C. exiguum*, Say.

Though these very little snails are terrestrial, yet, as they are attracted to the vicinity of water, their minute shells occur, often abundantly, in the alluvia of rivers. This species is common as a fossil of the Newer Tertiaries. Among the freshwater shells of the Purbeck beds at Villers-le-Lac, Doubs, there is a single species of land shell, *Carychium Brotianum*, the prototype of the genus.

GENUS CONOVULUS.

CONOVULUS DENTICULATUS—(*the Toothed Conovulus*) (Plate XI., fig. 134).—The shell is oblong, brittle, smooth, and of a brown or reddish-glossy colour; the spire is acute, with fine hairs around the sutures of the higher whorls; the aperture is oblong, rather thickened with three or five plaits or folds on the pillar, and a few denticulations on the outer lip; the length is about three and a half-lines, the width one and a-half. The lingual ribbon comprises twelve transverse rows, containing fifty-one teeth; the central tooth is short and rounded; the laterals at first are similar to the central tooth, but gradually merge into the uncini, which are short and bidentated.

The species varies considerably in size, colour, and length of spire, and number of teeth. A persistent variety is *C. myosotis* (Pl. XI., fig. 137); the shell is much thicker, and wants the tooth-like protuberances on the outer lip; it is a fossil of the Red Crag at Sutton, and of the Mammaliferous Crag at Bramerton, associated with an extinct species, *C. pyramidalis*.

C. denticulatus inhabits brackish marshes, or lives under stones immediately above high-water-mark, near the mouths of rivers, often in company with *Hydrobia ulvæ*. It also frequents the rejectamenta of rivers, feeding on the cast-up matter. The animal is active and irritable; it does not hibernate. Twelve eggs, or so, united into a common mass by a viscid material, are deposited among stones; they are hatched at the end of a fortnight, and the young attain the adult state in about a year.

The species is confined to the south and west shores of England, and is rare in Ireland. It is found in the interstices of a sea-wall in Portland Harbour, Maine.

CONOVULUS BIDENTATUS—(*the Two-toothed Cono-*

vulus) (Pl. XI., fig. 138).—The shell resembles that of the last, but is more oval, and of a yellowish, or brownish-white colour; it is more ventricose, and has only two plaits on the pillar. The foot is deeply transversely divided, whereas that of *C. denticulatus* is entire.   ·

Its habitats are the same as the last. It occurs in the south and west parts of England, and is pretty general along the Irish coasts.

OTINA OTIS, with a minute ear-shaped shell, is a marine species of the family *Auriculidæ;* it lives in the chinks of rocks at the margin of the sea in the south and south-west of Britain. The teeth resemble those of other *Pulmonata,* and are similar to *Conovulus.* There are ten rows of sixty teeth in each.

WATER SNAILS.

FAMILY LIMNÆIDÆ (*Water Air-breathing Snails*).

THIS very natural family comprises the fresh-water pulmoniferous snails; they all have short dilated muzzles, and two tentacles, with the eyes sessile at their inner bases. Nearly all the pulmonifera have only one jaw,* implanted superiorly between the lips; but species of the genera *Limnæa* (excluding *Amphipeplea*) and *Ancylus*, and *Planorbis corneus*, have three jaws or, more properly, the labial armature is formed of three pieces: the one large (the true jaw) is placed transversely above the mouth, whilst the other two, less in size, are placed vertically one on the right and one on the left side. In the remaining species the mouth is armed with a single arched piece. The lingual dentition presents widely distinct characters in the several genera. The stiff silky hairs, which are found on the skin of *Neritinæ*, have been found by M. Claperède to exist on most of our fresh-water

---

* This organ is composed of hardened mucus, and contains a feeble quantity of carbonate of lime.

mollusks.   Their shells are extremely variable,
spiral and turreted, dextral or sinistral, discoidal
and limpet-like; delicate, fragile, and of a uniform colour.   They have no operculum, but
secrete a thin epiphragm when the pools, in
which they live, dry up.

They inhabit fresh-water, at a small depth,
as they are compelled to rise frequently to the
surface to breathe; many of them can lower
themselves in the water by a glutinous thread.
They lay their eggs in a transparent jelly mass
on the leaves and stems of water plants, or on
stones.   The early development of a Pulmoniferous snail can be most conveniently observed
in a *Limnœa*.   In an aquarium, the eggs are
often deposited on the sides of the glass, and in
that case a microscope can be brought to bear
on the object, without at all interfering with the
course of nature.   The egg sacs are dull at the
moment of laying, but after remaining in the
water a few hours they become transparent.
The form of the albuminous mass varies somewhat with the species; it is usually an elongated
oval.   The eggs are hatched in about 30 days.
The snail is usually infested with a species of hair
worm (*Gordius inquilinus*), numbers of which
attach themselves around the neck and beneath
the tentacles, and are ever vibrating.   They are
falsely-parasitic, for they appear to derive no

sustenance from the snail, but feed on animal-cules.

From experiments made by Mr. Jennings and Dr. Ball, some of the water-snails appear to have the power of causing a peculiar sensation when placed on the tongue. The experimentalists operated upon the common pond-snail (*Limnæa peregra*); they allowed the foot of the animal to remain for a few minutes on the tongue, when the sensation was felt, varying in intensity according to the size of the animal, and the length of time it is allowed to remain. The sensation, though not decidedly painful, is yet rather disagreeable whilst it continues, frequently lasting from one to two hours, being exerted with greater energy during warm than cold weather. The same painful sensation was experienced by the contact of the river limpet (*Ancylus*) with the tongue. A few experiments were tried to ascertain whether the power arose from an acid secretion, capable of being emitted at pleasure by the animal, but so far without success. Have the pond-snails stinging or urticating organs of the nature of those which have been recently observed in the marine slugs (*Eolidæ*) ? ·

The family is represented in Great Britain by four genera, which may be distinguished as follows :—

Shell oval, spiral—
        (*a*) pillar with an oblique plait ...   ...   *Limnæa*
        (*b*) aperture sinistral   ...   .   *Physa*
Shell conical...   ...   .   *Ancylus*
Shell discoidal   ...   .   *Planorbis*

GENUS LIMNÆA (*Pond Snails*).

The generic word is derived from the Greek, *limne*, a marsh or pool.

The animal is of a greyish colour; the head is short and broad, with two flattened short triangular tentacles bearing eyes at their bases; the foot is broad and short, with two lobes, or simply notched in front. The jaw is composed of three smooth pieces; the superior one is usually produced in front to form a slight beak. The general character of the lingual ribbon is such as is represented in fig. 24.

The shell is spiral, oval, or oblong, thin, fragile, and translucent; the last whorl is large; the aperture is longer than wide, oval, with a thin edge and an oblique fold on the columella. They inhabit still and shallow waters, crawl slowly, float along the surface of the water with the foot, in the fashion of a boat, and the shell downwards, for the purpose of supplying themselves with air and collecting food. In a state of repose they adhere by their foot to stones and plants, and are capable of long immersion; in drought they partially bury themselves in the mud. The pond snails make a very audible squeaking noise on being taken out of the water. This arises from the expulsion of the water as the animal retreats within its shell.

The food of the pond snails is animal and vegetable matters in different states of putridity; they also feed on living aquatic plants, and the green confervæ encrusting their shells have been observed to be objects of attraction among themselves. Dr. Bland noticed that the water snails, by cleaning off the algal growth of the shells of their neighbours, removed the epidermis, or even made holes in them by this continued rasping; and thereby accounted for the decollation of the upper whorls of their shells, when not attributable to chemical agencies; formerly this propensity was regarded as one of true cannibalism, because, in the absence of other food, the snails devoured each other by piercing the shell at the apex, and eating away the upper parts of its inhabitant.

The water snails are very important elements in an aquarium, where the removal of decaying vegetable matter is necessary; they cannot, however, keep in check the confervoid growth.

Eight species of the genus are known in Great Britain, and are contained in three sections :—

I. *L. peregra, L. auricularia*, and *L. stagnalis,* have the last whorl much enlarged.

II. *L. palustris, L. truncatula,* and *L. glaber,* form another section, in which the spire is much elongated and the whorls gradually increase in size.

III. *L. glutinosa* and *L. involuta* are separated by some authors from the true pond-snails, and placed in a sub-generic group under the name of *Amphipeplea,* because they possess a globular membranaceous shell, and the animal, though like *Limnæa,* has the edges of the mantle, when the snail is in motion, extended so as to cover the shell.

A *Limnæa* is known in the Middle Purbecks, and the genus is represented by numerous species in the fresh-water beds of the Upper Eocenes, in the Isle of Wight; of the living species, *L. palustris, L. peregra,* and *L. truncatula,* first appeared during the deposition of the Mammaliferous Crag at Bramerton and Bulcham; they, with *L. stagnalis* and *L. auricularia,* occur in the Pleistocene marls of Essex.

LIMNÆA PEREGRA—(*the Wandering Mud Snail*) (Pl. X., fig. 117).—This mollusk is the most widely dispersed and abundant, and, at the same time, the most variable of the fresh-water snails.

The shell is ovate, thin, the colour varying

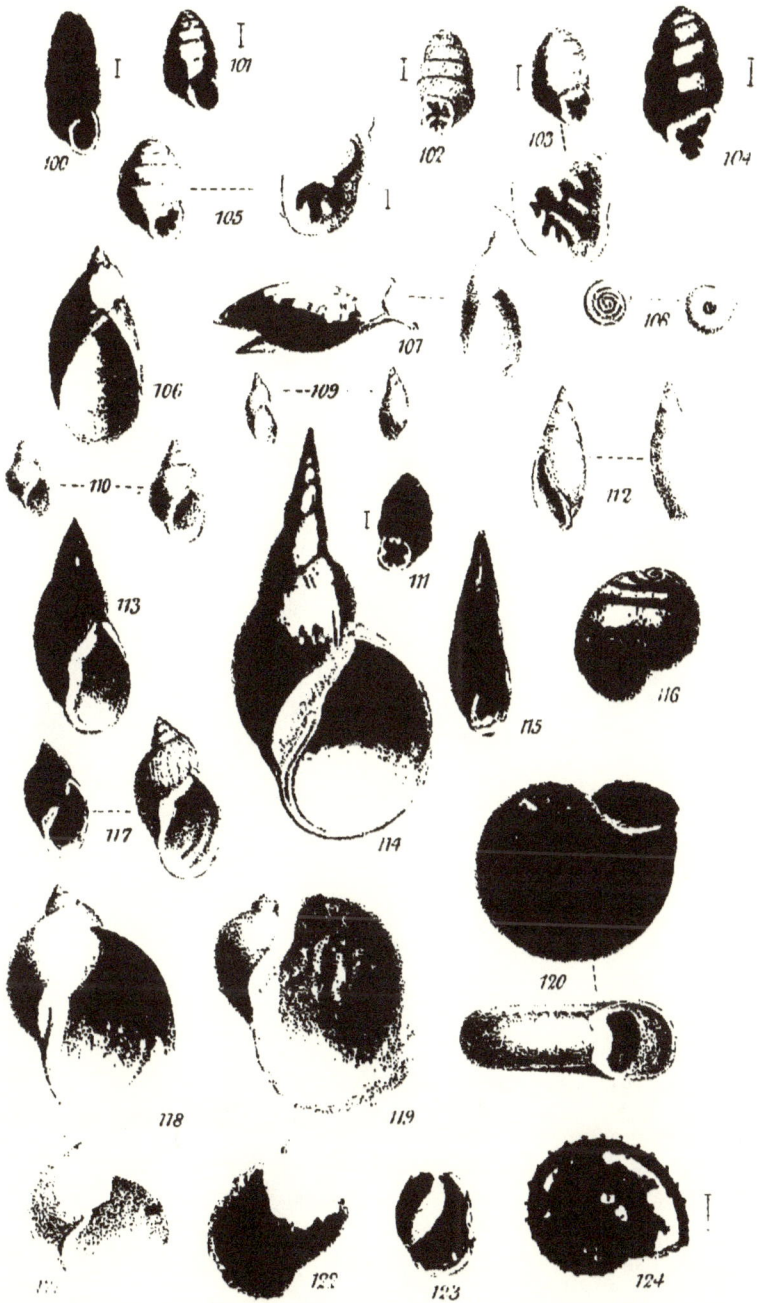

Plate X.

100

101

102

103

104

105

106

107

108

109

110

111

112

113

114

115

116

117

118

119

120

121

122

123

124

from a pale yellowish-grey to dark reddish-brown; under a high magnifying power the surface is seen to be striated spirally; the whorls are five in number, convex; the last one very large; the aperture is large and oval; the inner lip is folded on the columella, forming behind it a concealed narrow groove. The length is from half-an-inch to an inch; the breadth about two-thirds of the length.

The principal varieties which the shell of this species presents, are the following :—

1. *Var. ovata* (Pl. X., fig. 118).—The spire acute, extremely short; whorls exceedingly convex, the last very large; aperture obliquely produced, four-fifths of the whole length; shell very thin and glossy. It is thus distinguished by its ovate form, its dilated aperture, and acute spire. It attains a larger size than the normal form, and often equals the next species, *L. auricularia.* It is common, and is the form usually met with in still waters, especially if of great extent; whereas the smaller and narrower form—the type of the species—inhabits running waters, small brooks, and splashy pools.

2. *Var. lacustris* is an inhabitant of the mountain lakes in Scotland, Ireland, and North of England, and in the Shetlands. It has a small glossy thin shell, strongly concentrically wrinkled; the spire is very short, and the aperture is large;

this variety is intermediate in form between the typical *L. peregra* and *L. glutinosa*.

3. *Var. Burnetti* (Pl. X., fig. 116) differs from the type in its involute spire, placed more obliquely, in being regularly striated, and in the darker colour of the animal. This variety was detected by Mr. Burnett, in 1848, in the stomachs of trout caught in Loch Shene, and on a second visit he obtained many living examples. It occurs in a few other Scottish lakes and also in North Wales.

This species shows greater activity than the others of the genus; as implied by the specific name—from the Latin *peregrinor*, "to travel through strange places"—it is widely dispersed, everywhere abundant in ponds, ditches, and slow running water, and is not unfrequently found at some distance from the water, or walking on the moist mud. It attains an elevation of 1742 feet on the Aberdeenshire mountains.

It is very prolific, and lays upwards of a thousand eggs in a season; these are contained in clusters of from 12 to 100; the gelatinous mass in which they are imbedded is of an elongated oval form.

The dispersion of the fresh-water mollusks is chiefly effected by the agency of streams and and-floods; but wherever a pool of water is formed, *L. peregra* is the first to make its ap-

pearance, even in localities, such as a reservoir
on the top of a hill, where the ordinary agencies
will not account for its presence. Setting aside
the wonderful tales of " showers of snails," the
occurrence of shells in such localities is evidently
due to transportation by birds, the young snails
or capsules adhering to their feet. In elucida-
tion, here follows an experiment performed by
Mr. Darwin, and extracted from his " Origin of
Species" :—

"I suspended a duck's feet, which might re
present those of a bird sleeping in a natural
pond, in an aquarium, where many ova of fresh-
water shells were hatching; and I found that
numbers of the extremely minute and just-hatched
shells crawled on the feet, and clung to them so
firmly, that when taken out of the water they
could not be jarred off, though at a somewhat
more advanced age they would voluntarily drop
off. These just-hatched mollusks, though aquatic
in their nature, survived on the duck's feet, in
damp air, from twelve to twenty hours; and
in this length of time a duck or heron might fly
at least six or seven hundred miles, and would
be sure to alight on a pool or rivulet, if blown
across sea to an oceanic island, or to any other
distant point. Sir Charles Lyell also informs
me that a *Dytiscus* has been caught with an
Ancylus firmly adhering to it."

LIMNÆA AURICULARIA—(*the Wide-mouthed or Ear-shaped Mud Shell*) (Pl. X., fig. 119).—A large shell, and, without doubt, one of the most beautiful of the genus, remarkable for its globose form, and vastly expanded and roundish oval aperture; the spire is very short and acute; these characters serve to distinguish it from *L. peregra*. The shell is moreover beautifully glossy and semi-transparent; the lines of growth are deep and irregular. When the shell has lain dead for some time in the water, it becomes opaque, pale yellow externally and white within.

It has the habits of, but is less active than, the former species. It is local and rare; usually frequenting slow rivers, canals, and deep ditches; it is not uncommon in the valley of the Thames, and in low districts of the Eastern Counties; it has not been observed in Scotland.

LIMNÆA STAGNALIS—(*the Lake Mud Shell*) (Pl. X., fig. 114).—The shell of this species is larger and longer than that of any other *Limnæa*, being an inch and a-half long and nearly an inch wide; it is thin, brittle, of a greyish-white, brown or red colour; the spire is composed of six or seven rounded whorls, the last one occupying nearly three-fourths of the length of the shell. The shell varies in thickness, according to the nature of the water and food; in ponds, the last whorl is often much inflated; in clear running water, the shell is smaller, more slender, and tapering, and is the variety *fragilis;* though variable in its proportions, it always presents a very oblique aperture, exceeding in height half the length of the shell.

The dental formula of this species is $\frac{5.5 \cdot 1 \cdot 5.5}{1 1 0} =$ 12,210; the central tooth is very minute; the laterals are large with two unequal prominent points, the outer the smallest. (See fig. 24.)

Fig. 24.—Portion of a transverse row of the lingual ribbon of
L. stagnalis (Lovèn).

L. stagnalis prefers animal substances, and plays the part of "scavenger of the waters"; its presence in aquariums is almost necessary. It has been observed devouring the larva of *Dytiscus,* a water-beetle.

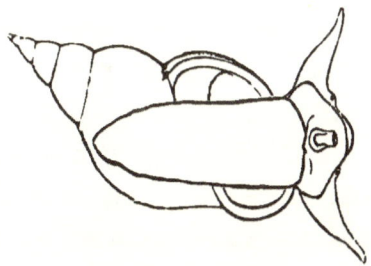

Fig. 25.—*L. stagnalis.*

It is a sluggish animal, and may be seen on a

summer's day traversing the surface of the water in an easy undulating line, or floating in luxurious repose, perhaps

> To taste the freshness of heaven's breath, and feel
> That light is pleasant, and the sunbeam warm.

When about to descend from the surface, it contracts the pulmonary pouch, expelling the air, and drops at once to the bottom, and regains the surface by crawling up some solid body.

This species is distributed throughout England, but is rare in the north; it inhabits Gulane Loch, 17 or 18 miles east of Edinburgh; it is rare in Ireland. The variety is found in a few canals. I have met with it very elongated in the River Lea, at St. Alban's.

L. stagnalis furnishes us with one of the problems of Natural History — its disappearance in localities where it has been more or less abundant for some years. Thus Dr. Johnston recorded the presence, and after a short lapse of time the total disappearance, of this snail in Berwickshire. Having observed this phenomenon in part, I am enabled to give the following probable explanation:—A pond in the neighbourhood of Hastings was tenanted by many adults of *L. stagnalis;* in the following year they were not to be found; but in the summer of the succeeding year I found them again in plenty.

Now this snail is a favourite food of ducks and geese, and the proximity of a farm, where these birds were kept, to the pond with *L. stagnalis* suggests to me the probable cause of their disappearance; but the eggs having escaped the general despoliation remained to replace their predecessors, and after the end of the first year attained to the adult condition. I had no opportunities of determining whether in the interval the pond was unfrequented by the geese, which appears somewhat necessary to account for the preservation of the young snails until they arrived at maturity.

In other districts, to call in the aid of the wild ducks and herons, which prey upon them, as the agents of extermination, is quite feasible.

LIMNÆA PALUSTRIS—(*the Marsh Mud Shell*) (Pl. X., fig. 113).—The shell of this species is oblong, conical, and pointed; colour, yellow to brown; whorls, six to seven, rounded, slightly convex, with a rather deep suture; the last whorl is large; the aperture is nearly half the length of the shell, purplish and glossy in the inside; the inner lip expanded, and partially covering the slight umbilicus; the maximum length is about three-fourths of an inch, but variable in size, as also in colour and form. Shells occur with spiral narrow white bands. Not unfrequently the spire is truncated or decollated from erosion or decay of the first whorls.

It is a common and generally distributed species, in ponds, marshes, and lakes, usually about their margins.

It differs from *L. stagnalis,* in the shell being thicker and the whorls narrower.

LIMNÆA TRUNCATULA—(*the Small Mud Shell*) (Pl. X., fig. 110).—The shell of this species differs from that of *L. palustris,* in its minute size, not exceeding half-an-inch in length, and in the more rounded and deeply separated whorls, somewhat abruptly bent towards the suture.

The above specific name, given to it by Müller, is derived from the truncated form of the whorls, and not from the decollation of the spire; for from its very habit it is not so liable to have the apex of its shell eroded. It received the name of *fossaria* from an English conchologist, Montagu, from its inhabiting ditches, and also that of *minuta* from Draparnaud, because of its diminutive size, it being the smallest of the genus.

L. truncatula is extremely variable in size, adult specimens being not unfrequently found one-third less in size than ordinarily; these inhabit high elevations and maritime marshes. It also presents very great differences in form, the degree of rugosity or smoothness, the pro-

minence of the spire and the outline of the
mouth.

This little mollusk is generally distributed
throughout Britain and Europe, and extends
into North Africa, Afghanistan, and Siberia. It
inhabits the banks of ditches, canals, muddy
streams, and rivers; it is found on the stones
of pools at considerable elevation on mountains,
where it is preyed upon by the lapwing;
it also frequents the moist mud and damp places
about springs and waterfalls. I have even taken
it in the rills at the margins of the high roads,
in which spots it was only occasionally bathed
in water, during and for a short time after rain.
L. truncatula, living as it does on the margins
of streams, pools, &c., differs in its habitats from
the species of the genus, which invariably pass
their days on submerged plants. In such spots
as indicated, this species deposits its eggs, which
are not fixed to the stems of aquatic plants, as
are those of its congeners, but are united in little
rounded masses, which rarely contain more than
from fifteen to twenty eggs.

In the heat of summer, the small mud-snails
bury themselves in the mud.

LIMNÆA GLABER—(*the Smooth Mud Shell*)
(Pl. X., fig. 115).—One of its synonyms is *L.
octona*, or "the Eight-Whorled Mud Shell."

The shell of this species is elongated, tapering,

composed of seven or eight rounded whorls, thin and glossy, but with a few faint longitudinal striations. The aperture is narrowed above, not a third of the length of the shell, with a thick broad white rib inside ; length of shell one inch

It is the rarest species of the genus, and is found in ditches and shallow pools in some of the eastern and south-western counties ; in marshes on the coast near Swansea ; in Yorkshire, Durham, and Staffordshire ; at Bowness, Westmoreland; in Ireland, Cork. It ranges into North and Central Europe.

LIMNÆA (AMPHIPEPLEA) GLUTINOSA—(*the Glutinous Membrane Shell*) (Pl. X., figs. 121, 122).— *L. glutinosa* differs from the species of the genus by the disposition of its mantle, which entirely covers the shell when the animal is submerged, and then resembles a ball of mucilage. It is this character which induced Nilsson to found a new genus, *Amphipeplea,* of it.

The shell of this beautiful and interesting mollusk is semi-globular, thin, transparent, and glossy amber-coloured ; the spire is very short, of three scarcely-produced whorls ; the length is about half-an-inch, and nearly as much wide. When the shell remains in the water after the death of the animal, it soon loses its transparency and beautiful amber colour.

The animal of *L. glutinosa* is large, glossy,

and nearly gelatinous, very broad, obtuse at its extremities. Its colour is greenish-yellow in the thin parts, but of greenish-grey in the denser parts. The foot is very large and truncated in front. The tentacles are extremely thin and transparent, slightly and irregularly veined with bright-grey. The jaw is single, composed of a slightly arched piece, with an indistinct median projection, and covered by numerous striations.

It is not by the mantle that the shell is covered, but by a simple dilatation of its border, which is entire and very contractile, and is pushed over upon the shell so as to envelop it like a bag. The protection thus afforded to the test is nearly always complete when the animals are immersed. In the larger individuals, when the water is deep and the sun shining, the mantle-expansions do not quite cover the upper surface of the shell, but a small round, oval, or irregular space is left, which enables one to see the speckled body. If the animal be disturbed by touching the edges of its sac, it endeavours to cover entirely the shell. The faculty of extension of the mantle margin is a gift of Nature, to counterbalance the extreme thinness and fragility of the shell.

The animals cannot live out of the water, and never voluntarily leave it; they are always on the move, especially during sunshine, but their walk is slow; they swim very well, with the shell inverted, at the surface of the water, which, if shallow and not sufficient, is soon rendered glutinous with their mucus threads.

The egg-masses are large, about two inches long, cylindrical, and slightly curved; the eggs are disposed in the capsules in two rows of about fifteen each, which are imbricated one on the other, but the length of the capsule, and consequently the number of eggs in each of them, are variable.

It occurs in ditches and lakes on aquatic plants, and is abundant, though very local. It is remarkable for its periodical appearance in the same spots. It is recorded, from the neighbourhood of Norwich on *Siums;* near Oxford; Dunster Castle, Somerset; Bala Lake, North Wales; and Windermere Lake; it ranges from Finland to the Pyrenees.

LIMNÆA (AMPHIPEPLEA) INVOLUTA—*(the Involute Membrane Shell)* (Pl. X., fig. 123).—It is easily distinguished from the last species by the sunken spire within the last whorl; the aperture of the shell is very large, and extends to the apex. The shell is small, polished, of a pale amber colour, extremely thin and membranous, as in *L. glutinosa,* with coarse longitudinal striæ; its maximum length is five and a-half lines, and its greatest breadth three and a-half lines.

This beautiful mollusk was discovered by Dr. Harvey, of botanical renown, in a small Alpine lake, and in a stream which flows into it, on Cromaglaun Mountain, near the lakes of Killarney in 1832; not the smallest trace of its existence in the many other tarns has been discovered. It is one of the very few pulmoniferous mollusks peculiar to Great Britain, which induced the late Professer E. Forbes to regard it as a probable monstrosity of *L. glutinosa*. Another point of interest regarding this snail, is that the shell partakes more of the form of the marine *Akera bullata* than of the other *Limnæas;* but the structure of the animal resembles that of other species of the genus. Accurate observations, however, are required to satisfactorily set at rest the disputed point as to whether the present species has expanded lobes to the mantle or not.

Dr. W. H. Evans communicated "An Ascent of Cromaglaun Mountain in Quest of *Limnæa involuta,*" to the "Naturalist," of November, 1864; from which I extract the following most complete account of the natural history of this species :—

"Its eastern side is almost overhung by the perpendicular wall of the higher ridge of the mountain, altogether precluding access in that quarter; the remainder of the lake being surrounded for the most part by bog. The water, impregnated by vegetable matter, is almost of a coffee colour, but generally clear, and the whole region has a wild and desolate aspect, strangely contrasting with the charming scenery we have just left. During the first quarter of an hour, I searched diligently on the leaves and stalks of the water-plants growing in the lake, and scooped up quantities of mud, which I carefully examined, but not a shell could I find. Water, rock, and mollusk were nearly of one colour; but by kneeling down beside the tarn, and putting my face almost close to the surface, I was able to see to some distance into the water. After gazing steadily for a few minutes, I thought I discovered two *Limnæas* crawling up the side of the rock, and a little careful manipulation with the scoop soon put me in possession of the prize. I spent about two hours at the lake, and took eleven specimens of the *Limnæa* in addition to the first, which the guide had broken, and in every instance the mollusk was either crawling on rocks or free; never attached to aquatic plants, or found in the mud. Had the day been bright and calm, I dare say I should have collected a greater number; but where the breeze rippled the surface of the water, it was impossible to see anything accurately, even at the depth of a few inches, unless it differed much from the

brown tint of the water. Owing to the un-
favourable state of the weather, and the con-
strained position I was forced to assume, it was
impossible to observe the animal very accurately
in the water; but although I looked for it, I was
unable to detect the mantle which is said to
cover the greater part of the shell. I kept them
in the box from Friday forenoon until late
on the following Monday evening; they were
then transferred to a tumbler of water, with a
little *Anacharis* in it, and they seemed as lively
and fresh as if they had been but an hour
caught. They moved about rapidly, and with a
continuous gliding motion over the sides of the
glass, sailing on steadily, so to speak, without
any of the jerking mode of progression so
common in most of the gasteropods. They
gradually died off, one surviving a fortnight.
During the time I had an opportunity of observ-
ing them in captivity I never could discover any
portion of the mantle expanded over the shell."

Genus Physa (*Bubble Shells*).

The animal is provided with two very long
slender tentacles, bearing the eyes at their bases
internally; the jaw is single and slightly arched;
the shell is sinistrally spiral, thin, and polished.
The two British species belong to two different

groups : *P. fontinalis* to the typical section, characterized by the oval shell ; the mantle is capable of being much extended, and its margins are fringed with long filaments ; *P. hypnorum*, belonging to the subgeneric section *Aplexa*, has an elongated spire, and the margin of the mantle plain.

Two species of *Physa*, the most ancient of the genus, are known in the Purbeck formation; many occur in Tertiary strata, and the two living species are fossils of the newer Tertiaries.

PHYSA FONTINALIS—(*the Stream Bubble Shell*) (Pl. XI., figs. 133, 141).—This pretty and interesting adjunct to an aquarium possesses an extremely thin, glossy, and semi-transparent shell of a yellowish or brownish colour, of an oval form, and nearly half-an-inch long, and about half as much broad; the whorls are four, the first three extremely small, the last one occupies three-fourths or four-fifths of the shell.

This species is widely distributed, and common on aquatic plants in brooks, ditches, canals, and slow-running rivers.

It exhibits great activity, and its modes of progression are various. The animal glides rapidly along with a uniform quick motion, its narrow and elongated foot apparently inadequate to support the bulky body. The head, which is obtuse in front, supports two long tapering and very slender tentacles; the eyes are situated at

Plate XI

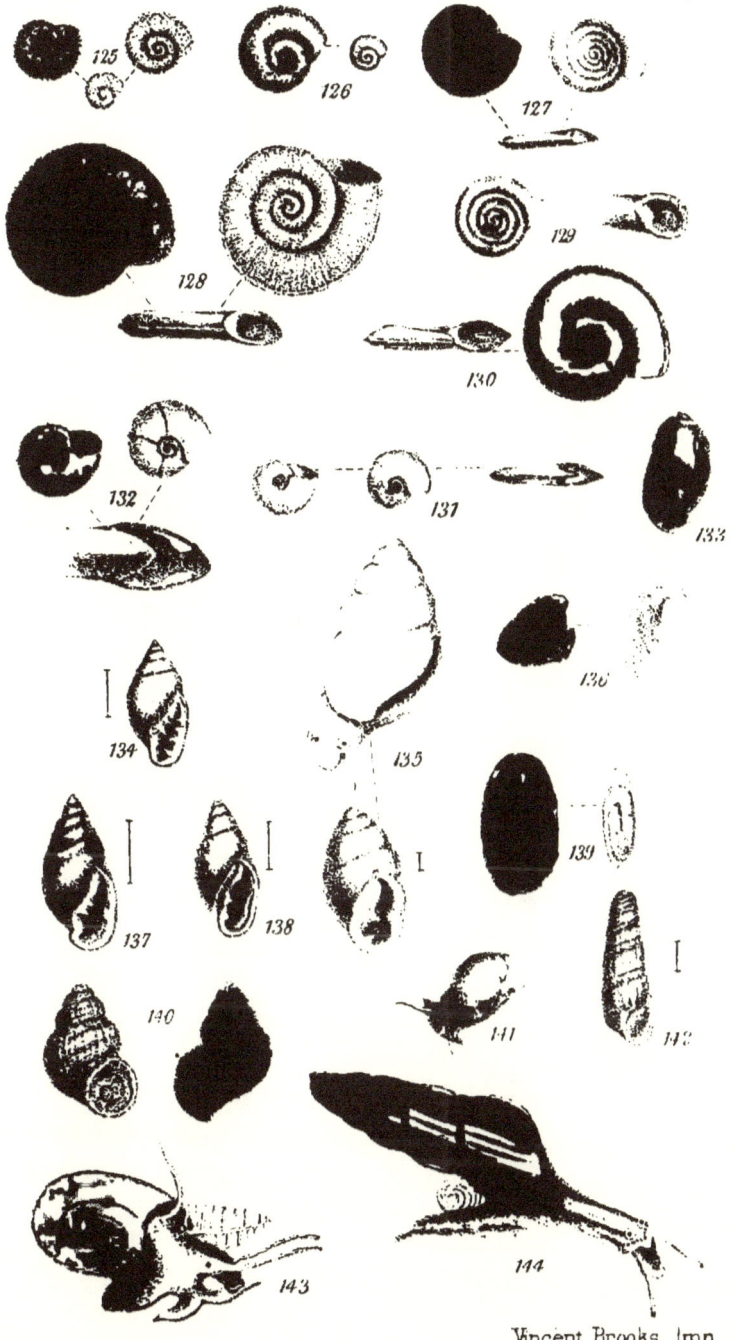

the inner bases of the tentacles, and are very conspicuous, their black colour contrasting strongly with the yellowish grey of the body. The edges of the mantle are extended into about twelve lobes, which can be spread over the shell, nearly meeting above.

This little *Physa* can raise itself in the water or sink at pleasure, without having recourse to plants to assist its progress; in descending through the water the movement is gradual and uninterrupted, and is effected by means of a thread affixed to the surface—a mode of progression analogous to that of some of the land slugs which I have referred to, as spinning a line of the gelatinous secretion from their skin; at other times it rises rapidly like a bubble from the bottom; it floats, walking along, as it were, immediately beneath the surface of the water by a series of jerks.

PHYSA (APLEXA) HYPNORUM—(Pl. X., fig. 112). —The inappropriate specific term signifies frequenting *Hypnum*, a genus of the mosses.

The shell of this species is easily distinguished by its elongated spire, and is half-an-inch or more in length, of a reddish colour.

P. hypnorum is very gregarious and prolific; it inhabits ponds and ditches, especially in the southern and midland counties of England; it occurs in Scotland and Ireland, but is local.

It is a very active creature, and ascends at will to the surface in a direct line, or returns to the bottom, or holds itself suspended in the water, with facility; its habits may be well observed in the aquarium. The above-mentioned movements of this snail are, according to Mr. J. Jones, effected in the following manner: "The edges of the foot are brought closely together, converting that member into a tube, from which the column of water therein enclosed is expelled with considerable force, either upwards or downwards, as the animal may be disposed to ascend or descend, being, in fact, a modification of the mode of locomotion adopted by the cuttle-fish, which effects its rapid movements by ejecting water through a funnel." The *Pisidiums*, the glass-bubble shell, and some of the pond-snails, as previously stated, exhibit the same powers; and it is the accepted explanation, that the snail does so by means of glutinous threads.

Mr. W. Nelson charges the present species with cannibalism; he writes, * * * * "on looking again, three or four days after, I found some more shells empty, but this time caught five or six of the real delinquents busily feeding on the dead body of one of their comrades, and one of the empty shells had a rather large hole in the whorl next to the body-whorl."

FRESH-WATER LIMPETS.

Genus Ancylus (*Fresh-water Limpets*).

This generic group is at once recognised by the conical, limpet-like, thin shells; the apex is posterior and sinistral. The animal is like *Limnœa*, but is more allied to *Planorbis*; its tentacles are cylindrical and not triangular. The mouth is armed with a jaw, composed of three rudimentary pieces. The lingual dentition presents the following characters: the central tooth is minute, the lateral teeth, thirty-seven in number, have long recurved hooks, and are at first simple, but becoming ultimately narrowed and minutely toothed; there are 120 transverse rows.

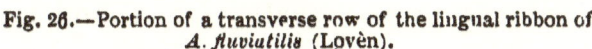

Fig. 26.—Portion of a transverse row of the lingual ribbon of *A. fluviatilis* (Lovèn).

In the subgeneric group, Velletia, *Gray*, the animal and shell are dextral; the lingual dentition is different, the central part of each row being much arched and composed of a central tooth with twelve similar laterals on each side; next to which is a tooth of a different form, and lastly, six more on each side, which latter are in a slight curve; the number of transverse rows is 75; the total number of teeth is 2,925.

To the type belongs *A. fluviatilis;* to the sub-genus, *A. oblongus;* both species occur fossilized in the newer Tertiaries. The genus *Ancylus* is represented by one species in the Middle Eocene of Hordwell.

ANCYLUS FLUVIATILIS—(*the River Limpet*) (Pl. XI., fig. 136).—The shell of the common "River Limpet" is an elevated and regular cone, with the point recurved and nearer the hinder end; it is thin, of a yellowish-grey or horn colour, the inside whitish and glossy; the exterior is ornamented with fine, close-set lines that diverge from the apex to the margin, but is more distinctly striated in the line of growth; the aperture of the shell is oval, and nearly a fourth of an inch in diameter; the height of the shell does not usually exceed half-an-inch.

The shell varies somewhat in form, some examples being proportionately larger and higher, others smaller and more swollen, and in the prominence of its ridges; in colour, varying from white to reddish-brown, and almost black. The shells are often coated with a brick-red ferruginous deposit. There is a pretty variety, with the interior of the shell of a violet colour, the aperture slightly elongated, and the epidermis of a deep colour.

The species is widely distributed through the length and breadth of Great Britain, and is abundant in brooks and in the shallow parts of rivers, fixed on stones or shells of fresh-water mussels, and rarely attached to aquatic plants. It is not unfrequently seen out of the water, on the moist surfaces of rocks by waterfalls; in such situations I have found the shells to be of an unusually small size.

I have never been able to witness the act of respiration in *Ancyli*, which appears to be only very rarely necessary, for the animals remain a very long time beneath the water, holding themselves with a perfect immobility to the submerged stones. However, it must not be supposed that such habits indicate any close affinity of *Ancylus* to the marine limpets (*Patella*); because, though the pond-snails frequently come to the surface to respire, the coil-snails do so much more rarely, and some Physas still less frequently perform the act. The fresh-water limpet was supposed to possess gills; and though since ascertained, beyond doubt, to be air-breathing, yet it is presumed to be capable of extracting air from the water, for the purpose of respiration.

Nevertheless, Mr. Clark suggests the following solution :—

" It is difficult to conceive how they can with safety come to the surface to breathe pure air, as, during the rainy seasons, the currents would probably drive such light and delicate animals down the stream, and cause them to perish, if they ventured to quit their moorings; they must, therefore, remain at anchor, unless they have the power, when they wish to breathe the pure air, of veering out a filamentary cable, by which they can withdraw again, after respiration, to their original site."

From their small size and sedentary habits the river limpets are not frequent denizens of our aquariums. The jelly-like egg masses of this species are attached to stones, and are ovate; they contain from four to eight eggs placed in a row. An annelid, *Matzia heterodactyla*, Vogt, lives in the mantle cavity of this species.

ANCYLUS (VELLETIA) OBLONGUS—(*the Oblong or Lake Limpet*) (Pl. XI., fig. 139). — This species, often termed *Ancylus lacustris*, or *Velletia lacustris*, is at once to be distinguished from the only other British species, *A. fluviatilis*, by its oblong shell, and by the form of the apex, which is twisted to the right, the shell being thus dextral. Dr. Gray regarded this difference of generic value, and constituted the genus *Velletia* for the reception of the present species. The shell is an elongated, subdepressed, and laterally compressed cone, of a light horn colour, and coarsely wrinked.

A. oblongus differs from the river limpet in its habitats; it lives attached to the under side of leaves and stems of aquatic plants, as the yellow water-lily (*Nuphar lutea*), *Alisma*, *Potamogetons*, and *Sparganiums*, and on the dead leaves of trees that have lain some time in the water; in still and gently flowing waters, as canals, lakes, and ponds.

The present species is more active than its ally; it glides quickly, with a perfect appearance of immobility in its plan of locomotion; but it may be observed turning its head from right to left, under the shell, during its march. The tentacles alone are capable of being extended beyond the shell; they are cylindrical, obtuse, slightly contractile, and, from their extreme tenuity, appear white; but, seen through a lens by the aid of sun-light, they are slightly tinged with black. The eyes can be seen by viewing the animal from the side; they are sessile, very large, and black, somewhat angular or rounded.

They never leave the water, and occupy themselves with cleaning off the green matter which is attached to submerged plants and bodies.

P

PLANORBIS (*Coil Snails*).

The shells of this genus are characterized as orbicular, flat, and coiled nearly in the same plane. The generic term signifies a flat coil. *Planus*, flat; *orbis*, coil or ball.

The animals inhabiting these discoidal shells are very slender, elongated, and twisted in a flat coil; they possess two very long and slender tentacles, the eyes situated at their inner bases. The foot is small; the lingual dentition is very simple : the transverse rows extend straight across the lingual membrane : the central tooth is generally two-pointed, the laterals with three points. The jaw is single and slightly arched (except in *P. corneus*), as in *Physa*, and in fact as in *Pupa*, *Balea*, *Clausilia*, and *Carychium*. The shells of this genus exhibit great tendency to distortion.

The species that compose this genus are numerous, inhabit slow running streams, ponds, and ditches, feeding on the aquatic plants, and are very sluggish in their movements. A peculiarity, possessed by all of the genus, may be readily observed by irritating the animal of *P. corneus* or *P. marginatus*, when a purplish liquid is emitted, which is not the blood, for the circulating fluid is colourless. The majority of the species are small: *P. nautileus* is the least, and *P. corneus* the largest of the British species. Monstrosities of the species occur with an elevated spire. The prevailing colour of the shell is greyish or reddish.

Coil shells are not known in a fossil state before the epochs of the Purbeck and Wealden deltas, two species of which occur in each of these formations. Species of *Planorbis* are among the most characteristic fossils of the Upper Eocenes of the Isle of Wight. Those at present living in this country are fossilized in the Upper Tertiaries of Grays, Clacton, &c., and at Clacton are associated with an extinct species, *P. helicoides*. *P. marginatus*, *P. spirorbis*, and *P. corneus* are the most ancient of the existing species; they occur in the Norwich Crag.

The British species are characterized as follows :—

1. { Whorls all exposed 2
{ Last whorl embracing the rest, glossy 10

2. { Whorls rounded 3
{ Whorls carinated 6

3. { Diameter long ... ... *P. corneus*
{ Shell small 4

4. { Whorls compact ... ... *P. contortus*
{ Last whorl proportionately large 5

5. { Shell covered with raised longitudinal striæ *P. albus*
{ Shell smooth ... ... *P. glaber*

6. { Shell very depressed, of many narrow whorls ... 7
{ Shell few-whorled ; last whorl rather large ... 8

7. { Shell very flat beneath, strongly keeled   ... *P. vortex*
   { Shell subcarinated   ... ...   *P. spirorbis*

8. { Shell very small, imbricated ridges   ...   *P. nautileus*
   { Shell large   9

9. { Keel on the middle of the whorl ...   ...   *P. carinatus*
   { Keel on the lower side ...   .   *P. marginatus*

10. { Bluntly keeled in the middle   ... ...   *P. nitidus*
    { Septa in the last whorl ...   .   *P. lineatus*

PLANORBIS CORNEUS—(*the Horny Coil Shell*) (Pl. X., fig. 120).—The shell of this species, the largest of the genus, is from half an inch to an inch in diameter; an unusually large specimen in my possession, from Tottenham, Middlesex, is an inch and a quarter across. The colour is a glossy, reddish-brown, sometimes white; the test thick and irregularly striated by curved lines of growth. The whorls are five in number, with a broad shallow umbilicus on the under side, the upper surface a little concave. The young shell has its surface of a velvety appearance, on account of the epidermis being clothed with a fine down.

The body is nearly black; the tentacles are long and curved. The jaw consists of three pieces, but the lateral ones are very rudimentary. A peculiarity of this animal, alike possessed by all the coil-shells, is that of emitting, when irritated, a purple-coloured fluid, which is secreted by a gland at the sides of its neck. It is a very sluggish animal, and on warm summer days may be seen floating in the water. When the ditches and ponds which it inhabits are dried up in the summer, the animal closes the mouth of its shell with a pellucid pellicle, and retires into the interior of its coil, and there remains in a state of torpidity until the ditches are again filled with water. This whitish filmy covering is analogous to the epiphragm of the land-snails, and is similarly pierced by a minute orifice, for the access of air for the purpose of respiration. To observe this epiphragm-like protection, take specimens of the *P. corneus* or any other species— *P. corneus* being the larger, the pellicle is more conspicuous—and place them in a dampish box, or a botanical box with a few moist aquatic plants; at the end of two or three days all the animals will be found to have taken this precautionary measure.

P. corneus is frequent in the ditches and ponds in the eastern counties of England; it is in great demand in the London markets for stocking aquariums; in other districts it is very rare. It occurs in a few localities in Ireland.

PLANORBIS CONTORTUS—(*the Contorted Coil Shell*) (Pl. X., fig. 108).—The shell resembles that of the last species in its rounded whorls, but is very small, not being more than two-tenths of an inch in diameter; the whorls are numerous and remarkably compact and narrow, nearly flat above, and with a large and deep umbilicus; the colour is bronzed-brown or horn; albino varieties occur. This minute snail possesses as many as 6,000 lingual teeth.

This is also a local species, though very abundant, when met with, living on water-plants in lakes, ponds, and ditches.

PLANORBIS VORTEX—(*the Flat Coil Shell*) (Pl. XI., fig. 127).—The shell is extremely depressed, thin, brown, pellucid, glossy; concave above, and flattish beneath, with from six to eight whorls; the outer whorl is rounded, but flattened underneath, so as to form a sharp keel or edge on the lower margin; the diameter of the shell is three-eighths of an inch.

This species is very generally diffused. It lives in shallow and stagnant waters, on the stems and leaves of plants, or floating on the surface, and rarely residing at the bottom. Its modes of progression are various, and very characteristic of the Coil Snails. It slowly glides along the surface of a leaf by extending its foot, and producing in it undulatory movements, by means of which it is propelled forward. Now and then, the shell, which is usually carried inclined at an angle of from 20° to 30°, is suddenly jerked forward by a semi-rotatory movement. Often the snail moves along with a continuous progress, without jerking the shell at intervals. Sometimes the shell is laid flat, kept at an angle of 50° or 60°, or even raised so as to be perpendicular. When swimming along the surface of the water, the shell lies flat on the surface.

PLANORBIS SPIRORBIS—(*the Round-edged Coi Shell*) (Pl. XI., fig. 129).—The shell of this species is very closely allied to that of *P. vortex,* from which it differs in being thicker, less flat, the whorls rounder, and the keel less distinct. Its habits are similar to those of *P. vortex.*

It is more widely diffused than the last.

PLANORBIS MARGINATUS—(*the Flattened Coil Shell*) (Pl. XI., fig. 128).—The shell is of a brownish colour, with close irregular striations, concave above, and flat or slightly convex below; whorls, six; the diameter of the last whorl is equal to about one-fourth of the whole, and is rounded above, and strongly keeled below. In the young, the *P. rhombœus* of Turton, the shell is more convex above, and with a deep concavity beneath, and a blunt keel. Monstrosities of this species occur with the volutions elevated into a spiral cone, as in fig. 27; or with the first few whorls coiled in the normal way, the others spiral; or with open whorls.

Fig. 27.

This snail is prolific, and lays from eight to ten capsules, each containing from six to twenty eggs.

It can fix its shell without any apparent means of attachment by its side to the flat surface of the aquarium glass, where it may be often found left high and dry by the loss of water in the glass by evaporation. The flattened coil shell, so frequent in the ponds and ditches of the south and midland counties of England, becomes rare northwards, and is unknown in Scotland; it occurs throughout Ireland.

A well-known synonym of this species is *P. complanatus.*

PLANORBIS CARINATUS—*(the Keeled Coil Shell)* (Pl. XI., fig. 130).—The shell differs from that of the last in its broader and more depressed whorls, and the keel being situated on the middle line of the whorl instead of below. It is of much rarer occurrence, and never plentiful. It is found somewhat generally in the eastern counties; it is doubtfully Scottish, but occurs in Ireland.

PLANORBIS ALBUS—*(the White Coil Shell)* (Pl. XI., fig. 125).—The specific name *albus* is applied to this species from the greyish-white colour of the animal and shell. The head of the snail is thick and oblong in front, the tentacles are long, slender, of a pale grey or white, with a central brown line, dilated and transparent; at the base on the inner side of each tentacle is a small oval black eye. The foot is narrow, the length of which is about one-third the diameter of the shell. The animal, when walking in the water, carries the shell inclined at an angle of from 70° to 80°.

The shell is finely striated longitudinally; the epidermis is raised into deciduous bristles on the striations, also minutely striated transversely; convex above and below, thin, pellucid, and whitish; about one-fourth of an inch in diameter; the whorls five, the last one disproportionately enlarged.

It is a common species.

PLANORBIS GLABER—(*the Smooth Coil Shell*) (Pl. XI., fig. 126).—The nearest ally to this species is *P. albus*, from which it differs in its smaller shell, which is smooth; in the more rounded whorls, the upper side being more convex; and, lastly, in being destitute of the strong spiral striæ.

P. glaber was first described by Mr. Jeffreys, who states that he only knows about twenty localities for it in England and Scotland; it is rather a northern than a southern form; it has been found in the neigbourhood of Belfast, Ireland, and in three other localities in the northeast of the island. It is distributed throughout the greater part of the continent, and ranges from Sweden to Corsica and Algeria.

PLANORBIS NAUTILEUS—(*the Nautilus Coil Shell*)

(Pl. X., fig.124).—This is the most elegant and at the same time the smallest of our fresh-water mollusks. The shell bears some general resemblance to that of *P. albus;* but its minute size, dull appearance, and, above all, its sculpturations, serve to distinguish it. It máy be described as —flat, rather concave in the middle, lower side rather convex, thin, pellucid, dull, light-brown or grey; the whorls three, the last one enlarged, strongly marked with transverse ridges, which are more marked ' in young individuals; the diameter is two-twelfths of an inch.

The species is known by another name, *P. imbricatus,* perhaps more characteristic than the one adopted, which, however, has the priority.

P. nautileus is widely distributed, but is not a common species.

The readiest plan to secure this species and other minute fresh-water shells, is to collect the confervæ and plants on which they live, place them in a basin, and pour warm water on them; the animals will then relinquish their hold and fall to the bottom.

PLANORBIS NITIDUS—(*the Shining Coil Shell*) (Pl. XI., fig. 131).—This and the following species are associated together from the glossy aspect of their shells, and from the last whorl being very large in proportion to the rest, and more or less embracing them. The shell of *P.*

nitidus is depressed, the upper more convex than the lower side; of a dark horn colour, very glossy, semi-transparent; the whorls are four in number; the diameter of the shell is two and a half lines; the outer whorl exceeding the rest in size, with a blunt keel in the middle.

This small and pretty mollusk is not frequent, though dispersed throughout the British isles; it may be obtained generally on the fallen leaves of trees, also on aquatic plants in ponds and ditches.

PLANORBIS LINEATUS—(*the Streaked Coil Shell*) (Pl. XI., fig. 132).—The shell of this species closely resembles that of the last, but is of a lighter colour, thinner, flatter, the keel sharper, and the last whorl not so embracing; it is markedly distinguished by the presence of from two to five curved transverse plates inside the last whorl; on the exterior these septa appear as whitish lines. This peculiarity of structure induced Lightfoot, in 1786, to call this shell a *Nautilus;* and subsequently Dr. Fleming regarded the presence of the plates as sufficient to raise it to the rank of a genus, under the name *Segmentina.*

The present species is the rarest of the British fresh-water mollusks; it is found chiefly in the neighbourhood of London and in the adjacent districts; it occurs in the co. Tipperary, Ireland; and is distributed throughout Central Europe.

OPERCULATED LAND SHELLS.

ORDER OPERCULATA.

THE Operculated Snails closely resemble the plant-eating gasteropods, as *Bithinia* and the periwinkle; and chiefly differ from them in their habitats and the medium they respire. They have a long muzzle, two slender tentacles, contractile, but not retractile, like those of the *Helicidæ*; the eyes are sessile. The lingual ribbon differs very widely in the aspect of its teeth from the land-snails, and is narrow. The teeth are large; three on each side of a central tooth, and thus they very much resemble those of the fluviatile gasteropods. The sexes are distinct; the aperture of the shell is closed by an operculum.

The order contains two families, each with a single representative species in Great Britain; they may be distinguished as follows:—

Shell oval ; operculum shelly...   ...   ... *Cyclostoma elegans*
Shell cylindrical ; operculum horny   ...   ...   *Acme fusca*

CYCLOSTOMA ELEGANS — (*the Elegant Circle-mouthed Shell*) (Pl. XI., fig. 140).—The shell is about a fourth of an inch long, and four-tenths wide, solid, of a grey or purplish yellow, with two or three rows of darker spots; the whorls are five in number, rounded, and strongly striated spirally; the aperture is circular, slightly angular above, and closed with a hard shelly operculum.

The inhabitant of this beautiful shell has a very striking appearance (see fig. 28); the muzzle projects far beyond the body, and is used to

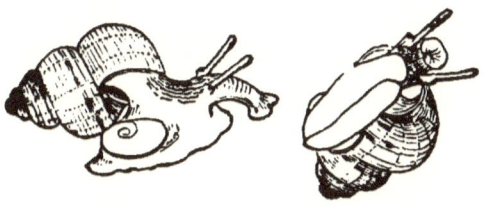

Fig. 28.—*Cyclostoma elegans.*

assist the snail in climbing; the tentacles are annularly wrinkled, and terminated by brown bulbs; the eyes, in place of being situated at the extremity of the upper tentacles, as in the majority of the terrestrial mollusks, are placed on each side of the head at the bases of the tentacles; the foot is short and broad, and divided in its length by a groove; when the animal walks, the portion on the one side is advanced, the animal retaining its hold by the other, and then holds on by the advanced portion as the other is gradually brought in advance of it. "This species present a most remarkable peculiarity in its anatomy, that of a brilliant white organ lodged among the convolutions of the intestine; it contains a multitude of solid concretions, composed of an organized skeleton and incrusting salts." (Claparède.)

This species is abundant in the localities where it is found, but is always confined to calcareous soils, especially those of the oolites and chalk. It dwells in hedge-rows and on the margins of woods, or more rarely on open downs and hills. It ranges as far north as Yorkshire, is absent in Ireland and in Scotland, and is distributed over Central and Southern Europe, and extends to the Canaries and Algeria.

The restriction of this species to limestone soils is very marked. It occurs throughout the whole of the chalk and oolitic ranges in great abundance, more sparingly on the Mountain Limestone hills. Dr. S. P. Woodward informs me, that in Norfolk it is found in great profusion on the bosses of chalk that appear among the overlaying Tertiary gravels and clays, and is not met with in the intervening areas. Notably also, the junction of the chalk with the low alluvial plains in the Wealden district is very accurately indicated by this shell. Thus, although the hilly districts of the Hastings Sands apparently seem favourable to the existence of this snail, it does not occur there, nor upon the plains of alluvium and weald clays that stretch up to the base of the chalk downs of Eastbourne on the west, and those of Kent on the east; but on passing on to the chalk it is met with in extraordinary numbers.

In Gloucestershire, shells of this species constitute a stratum, at a depth of 6 or 9 inches beneath the surface, that I have traced over several square miles. In the Isle of Wight and in Dorsetshire it is found similarly in a subfossilized state.

ACME FUSCA—(*the Brown Acme*) (Pl. XI., figs. 142, 144).—The shell is scarcely one-tenth of an inch long, cylindrical, and very polished; under a good lens it is seen to be marked with distant longitudinal striations; the colour is glossy brown; the aperture is roundish oval, contracted above and closed with a thin horny-whitish operculum; the whorls six or seven; the umbilicus is small.

It is rare in Great Britain, but widely distributed. It lives among decaying leaves and tufts of moss, in moist situations, especially near the sea. I was once successful in securing several living specimens of this minute species, by collecting dead leaves and shreds of bark into a heap; and upon turning over the mass, after a lapse of a few weeks, my heart was gladdened with the much-prized treasures and many other interesting species. The above kind of bait I have employed very frequently and found it to answer extremely well, naturally so, as it affords food, shelter, warmth, and moisture to the snails.

A. fusca is known in a fossilized state at Copford, Essex.

EXPLANATIONS TO THE PLATES.

Q

* The spire is too elevated, and the mouth too circular.
—R. T.

Q 2

INDEX.

I.

P.

Planorbis rhombeus, 215.
—— spirorbis, 215.
—— vortex, 214.
Pomade and syrup of snails, 115.
Pond snails (Limnæa), characters of, 184 ; food of, 185 ; species and geological distribution of, 186.
Posterior margin, 11.
Preparation of lingual ribbons for microscope, 49.
Preserving bivalves, 20 ; slugs, 90 ; land snails, 98.
Protozoan animals, 2.
Pulmoniferous animals, 3.
—— snails (class Pulmonifera), 65.
Pupa, characters of, 152 ; synoptical list of species of, 153 : geological distribution of, *ib.*
—— Anglica, 155.
—— muscorum, 154.
—— secale, 157.
—— umbilicata, 153.
—— vestuta, 153.

R.

Radiating lines on shells, 45.
Reflected lip of shells, 45.
Reproduction of bivalves, 18 ; of water-breathing snails, 52 ; of land snails, 94.
Respiration in bivalves, 15 ; in water-breathing snails, 52 ; in air-breathing snails, 65 ; in *Ancylus fluviatilis*, 207.
Reversed shells, 45.

S.

Scoop for collecting, 19.
Secretion of colour in shells, 46.
Segmentina lineata, 219.
Sense of hearing and sight in bivalves, 17 ; water-breathing snails, 52.

U.

V.

W.

Z.

THE END.

COX AND WYMAN, PRINTERS, GREAT QUEEN STREET, W.C.

Sowerby's English Botany:

Containing a Description and *Life-Size* Drawing of every British Plant.   Edited and brought up to the present standard of scientific knowledge by T. Boswell Syme, F.L.S., &c.   With Popular Descriptions of the Uses, History, and Traditions of each Plant, by Mrs. Lankester, Author of "Wild Flowers worth Notice," "The British Ferns," &c.   The Figures by J. E. Sowerby, James Sowerby, F.L.S., J. de C. Sowerby, F.L.S., and J. W. Salter, A.L.S.

The Distinctive Characteristics of this edition are,—

1. A life-size drawing of every British plant, arranged according to the Natural System of De Candolle.

2. Where necessary, the plates are accompanied by illustrations of the structure of the various organs of the plant, especially of those structures discovered within the last few years by the use of the microscope.

3. All the illustrations are full-coloured, instead of half-coloured, and the utmost care is taken to adhere as closely as possible to nature.

"Under the editorship of T. Boswell Syme, F.L.S., assisted by Mrs. Lankester, whose work on 'Wildflowers worth Notice' is so well appreciated by the public, we have the best guarantee that 'Sowerby's English Botany,' when finished, will be exhaustive of the subject, and worthy of the branch of science it illustrates. . . In turning over the charmingly executed hand-coloured plates of British plants which encumber these volumes with riches, the reader cannot help being struck with the beauty of many of the humblest flowering weeds we tread on with careless step. Our fields, woods, and hillsides, are paved with riches we all too much neglect. . . We cannot dwell upon many of the individuals grouped in the splendid bouquet of flowers presented in these pages, and it will be sufficient to state that the work is pledged to contain a figure of every wild flower indigenous to these isles."—*The Times,* Nov. 3, 1865.

"Will be the most complete Flora of Great Britain ever brought out.   This great work will find a place wherever botanical science is cultivated, and the study of our native plants, with all their fascinating associations, held dear."—*Athenæum.*

"Nothing can exceed the beauty and accuracy of the coloured figures.   They are drawn life-size—an advantage which every young amateur will recognize who has vainly puzzled over drawings in which a celandine is as big as a poppy—they are enriched with delicate delineations of print, petal, anther, and any organ which happens to be remarkable in its form—and not a few plates are altogether new. . . . .   A clear, bold, distinctive type enables the reader to take in at a glance the arrangement and divisions of every page.   And Mrs. Lankester has added to the technical description by the editor, an extremely interesting popular sketch, which follows in smaller type. The English, French and German popular names are given, and, wherever that delicate and difficult step is at all practicable, their derivation also.   Medical properties, superstitions, and fancies, and poetic tributes and illusions follow.   In short, there is nothing more left to be desired."—*Guardian.*

"Should the succeeding parts be as good, the work, when complete, will be without a rival in excellence."—*Observer.*

"Without question, this is the standard work on Botany, and indispensable to every botanist. . .   The plates are most accurate and beautiful, and the entire work cannot be too strongly recommended to all who are interested in Botany."—*Illustrated London News.*

LONDON: ROBERT HARDWICKE, 192, PICCADILLY.

The Useful Plants of Great Britain.

A Treatise on the Principal Native Vegetables capable of Application as Food or Medicine, or in the Arts and Manufactures. By C. P. JOHNSON. Illustrated by J. E. SOWERBY. 300 Illustrations coloured by hand.

A Manual of Structural Botany.

By M. C. COOKE, Author of "Seven Sisters of Sleep," &c.

"Condensed yet clear, comprehensive but brief, it affords to the learner a distinct view."—*Globe.*

"We are confidently able to recommend the little volume to public favour, its very low price (1s.) bringing it within the range of all purchasers."—*Era.*

A Manual of Botanic Terms.

By M. C. COOKE. With more than 300 Illustrations.

"We do not hesitate to say that by a careful use of this book a sound knowledge of the theoretical portion of Botany may be obtained without tedious labour."—*Mining Journal.*

The Fern Collector's Album.

A Descriptive Folio for the reception of Natural Specimens; containing on the right-hand page a description of each fern printed in colours, the opposite page being left blank, for the collector to affix the dried specimen; forming, when filled, an elegant and complete collection of this interesting family of plants.

Size of the Small Edition, 11¾ by 8½ in.; Large Edition, 17¼ by 11 in.

The British Ferns

(A plain and Easy Account of). Together with their Classification, Arrangement of Genera, Structure, and Functions, Directions for Out-door and In-door Cultivation, &c. By MRS. LANKESTER.

"Not only plain and easy, but elegantly illustrated."—*Athenæum.*

"Mrs. Lankester has given us a handy pocket volume, with a great deal of information about the uses, supposed and real, of the Ferns, and hints for their cultivation."—*Guardian.*